Frontier Boundaries

Terri Downes

Published by Trellis Publishing, 2021.

This is a work of fiction. Similarities to real people, places, or events are entirely coincidental.

FRONTIER BOUNDARIES

First edition. July 13, 2021.

ISBN: 979-8224065264

Written by Terri Downes.

FRONTIER BOUNDARIES

TERRI DOWNES

FRONTIER BOUNDARIES

"What do you think you're doing?"

The man jumped at the sound of Morgan's voice, lowering his rifle before turning to face her. She supposed he had not heard her horse approaching over the noise of his shots, as he looked very surprised.

"I said what do you think you're doing?" Morgan shouted again.

The man looked over to where he had lined up some empty tin cans on a low ridge of rocks, then back at Morgan.

"Well, I *think* I'm shooting cans," he said slowly. "Does it look like I'm doing something else?"

Morgan barely felt the ground under her feet as she leapt down from her horse. The man stared at her as she marched up to him and stood a couple of feet away with her hands planted on her hips.

"This isn't your land," she said.

The man raised an eyebrow.

She opened her mouth to say something else – *you'd better get moving – watch where you're headed next time – you could have shot someone by accident* – but as she looked at the man directly, her thoughts suddenly tripped over themselves and she was unable to get the words out.

She could see now that he was smiling slightly, presumably over his attempt at a joke. It was a small, lopsided smile, his eyes sparkling above it with a light defiance.

"I know it's not my land, but I didn't think it was anyone else's," the man said, holstering the rifle.

Morgan swallowed against the sudden dryness in her throat as she met his eyes.

"It's my family's land," she informed him. "Those are our boundary markers over there."

The man looked at where she was pointing. Morgan shook herself, trying to fight the sudden flustered feeling that had come over her.

There was no reason to feel flustered, she told herself. She was the one in the right.

"How is anyone supposed to notice a line of rocks along the ground?" the man said. "At least put a sign up or something."

"Everyone knows this is our land," said Morgan.

The man raised his eyebrows. Looking directly into his eyes – clear, dark, and honey colored as they were – suddenly seemed like too much of a challenge. Morgan lowered her gaze to somewhere near his throat.

"I didn't know, so obviously that's not true." The man shrugged. "But I'll clear off if it's such a problem."

"You're not going to apologize?"

"For what?"

Morgan now found looking at the man's throat distracting as well.

He had a slender build, but strong, she thought, and she could see the movement of his shoulders beneath his shirt, the way they led up into the lines of his neck, giving off some sense of vitality that she could not define.

"For trespassing," she said. She held her head high, trying to show him who was in charge here – but also in an attempt to look at the top of his head, which was all she could think to do with her eyes wandering all over the place.

"Put up a fence if you're so worried about trespassers." The man looked behind Morgan, toward the low hills where her family home lay. "So this is... the Sullivan Ranch, I guess?"

"Yes," said Morgan stiffly. "You're new here?"

"Hardly," grinned the man. "You don't recognize the shopkeepers from around town, I suppose."

Morgan flushed. She knew hers was the only really wealthy family in the area, and that some people would probably think they were snobs. And maybe they were, but it was hardly something to comment on.

"That depends what they sell," she returned, nodding at the rifle. "You sell guns?"

"How observant you are," grinned the man, and Morgan had to look away again.

"There's no need to mock me," she said to the air over his left shoulder. "I'm not being unreasonable. You know it's our land now, so you need to go. "

"Sure, sure, I'll go," said the man. He did not turn away, but instead looked Morgan up and down. "And never was such as curt message delivered by such a beautiful messenger."

Morgan's mouth fell open.

"I beg your pardon?"

"You heard." The man looked completely unrepentant.

"What on earth do you mean by that? " Morgan demanded.

"I could stay and explain it to you if you'd like," said the man, tilting his head to one side.

Morgan felt as though someone had dropped a stone into her stomach as the man's smile opened up fully. She stared at it for a moment, the sounds of the pasture around them growing loud in the silence.

As the man shifted slightly, looking as though he were about to speak again, Morgan managed to turn away and started walking back her horse. The ground felt as though it was turning to liquid beneath her feet.

"Suit yourself," the man called after her.

Morgan did not look back as she started to ride away, knowing that he would see. But once she had made it a few hundred yards, she could not stop herself from twisting around in the saddle to stare after him for a moment.

He had cleared the cans away and was heading back toward town, walking at a leisurely pace, head tilted up as though he were gazing at the sky.

Morgan looked back as long as she dared, then headed once more for home.

She could still feel her heartbeat all the way along her limbs, throbbing at her fingertips.

And this was a problem. Because she could not remember ever feeling this way before. Not with any man she had ever met.

Certainly not with her fiancé.

*****

When Robert heard that there was some party up at the Sullivan's place, his first reaction was to wonder whether his comments had had an effect on that daughter of theirs, the one who had shouted at him last Tuesday. Morgan was her name, he had remembered, but only after he had made it home.

She had looked offended when he had hinted she would not know the townspeople in Lawson – actually offended, not that false offense she had put on when Robert had told her she was beautiful.

He almost laughed when he thought of his little compliment. The girl probably thought he was some die-hard flirt, and would have no idea that that was the first time he had spoken to a woman like that since – well, since Joanna.

Miss Sullivan had started it, after all, coming up and looking him all over as though he was something in a shop window. And then acting so innocent when he returned the attention, honestly.

At any rate, Robert had been invited with all the other business owners and their families, and saw no reason to decline. This would be one of the first social events he had been to since moving here. His sister Ruth had often hinted in her letters that he should get out more, but he had never really had a reason to go before.

Robert paused at this thought, as he reached the Sullivan place. He let Mr Green, the owner of the general store with whom he had ridden up, dismount ahead of him as he looked ahead at the house.

Was that his reason for being here? Seeing the girl again – was that all? Because seeing her was all he could hope for. Nothing else.

Then he caught a glimpse of Morgan, standing beside her parents at the door of the house, greeting the guests as they arrived. She looked over at him, and suddenly became entirely still, although her genteel expression remained in place.

Robert smiled to himself. Yes, this was as good a reason as any.

He wondered, as he approached, whether she was going to pretend that she didn't recognize him. But as he was introducing himself to the Sullivans, her cool voice could be heard:

"Mr Cole is the gunsmith in town," she said with a tone that suggested she knew *everyone* there was to know in the local stores and businesses.

Robert waited until her parents had looked away, moving to meet the next guest, before grinning at Morgan.

"Where did you learn my name?" he asked quietly.

"Maybe I'm very well informed," she said.

Then she glanced over at her parents and returned his smile, just for a moment. *Oh, she's done pretending,* Robert thought.

"Or maybe my fiancé told me," she added casually.

She nodded over at a corner where a tall, well-groomed young man was standing, talking to one of the town bankers. Robert could feel Morgan's eyes on him, waiting for him to react. Was she expecting him to look downcast, or betrayed, at discovering she was engaged? Fine chance of that.

She was done pretending; she just wanted to start a new game.

"How nice to have a well-informed fiancé," Robert said placidly. "You'll save so much money on almanacs."

A dark look flashed across the girl's face, but she quickly balanced it with another smile.

"Maybe I'll go and mingle a little," said Robert, wanting to be the first one to break their tête-à-tête. "Never hurts to make friends."

"That depends who the friend is," said the girl, turning away before Robert had the chance to.

He watched her walk off before moving himself, knowing she would be able to feel his eyes on her.

***

Morgan wished she had not told Mr Cole about Geoff so soon. All through dinner, every time Geoff spoke to her, she had to fight the compulsion to turn and look at Mr Cole. Sometimes she could not help herself, and she would look – he would almost always be looking away, and then would turn and catch her staring, smiling with a slight air of triumph.

But sometimes, he would already be looking at her, and she would have the right to a triumphant expression.

It annoyed her at first that he refused to behave as though he should, after losing a point; he would simply smile back before turning away again. But then she started doing the same thing, and by the end of dinner it felt as though she had been place tennis across the table for an hour.

It did not help matters that she had to keep hiding the looks and smiles from Geoff – and from everyone else present. Fortunately, there were a couple of very loud gentlemen near the middle of the table who were entertaining everyone with a winding tale of an excursion they had taken to Europe a few years back.

And when Mr Cole found her later in the evening – over and over, a moment here and a few words there – Morgan could not help but return his little jokes, his looks, drinking in the way his eyes lingered on her as though his attention was made from honey.

It doesn't matter, she told herself, over and over throughout the evening. *It doesn't mean anything, he knows it can't go anywhere. He knows about Geoff.*

She told herself this so firmly that when she saw Mr Cole standing out on the back porch by himself – late in the evening, as everyone was starting to say their goodbyes – she didn't hesitate before going out to join him.

She did hesitate for just a moment as she reached him, realizing that she was probably standing too close, and that someone might come out and see them. But when she glanced behind her, and then looked back, Mr Cole once more had that look of triumph about him, and she refused to budge.

"Have you enjoyed your evening?" Morgan asked, allowing her voice to stay quiet in the small space between them.

"Tremendously," he said. "I don't know when I've felt so welcomed."

"We like everyone to feel welcome here," smiled Morgan.

"Really? Then why do I feel like I've been getting special treatment?"

He really was standing very close, Morgan thought. Or she was standing very close to him. Or something.

Maybe she was pushing this too far. She had not flirted with anyone since getting engaged – and even before, it had never been like this, never with this sense of being unable to stop.

She should have better control over herself.

"You know I'm engaged," she said suddenly.

"You mentioned it."

"Geoff is a wonderful man."

"I'm sure he is," said Mr Cole. "And very lucky."

Neither of them moved.

"I did tell you about the importance of setting up proper boundary markers," said Mr Cole, as Morgan found herself staring at his mouth again.

"And what do you mean by that?" asked Morgan, knowing exactly what he meant.

"I mean that with you standing here like this, it might seem like an invitation," said Mr Cole.

This was her signal to walk away, Morgan knew.

When she didn't, she knew what was going to happen.

***

The thrill of leaning forward into the half-dark and stealing a kiss when there were so many chances of getting caught felt almost as good as the kiss itself, Robert thought. Almost.

As he broke away from Morgan, he wondered for a moment if she was going to react poorly – maybe he had misread her – but she didn't. She stayed still for a second, and then they both moved away from one another as they heard someone moving inside, near the porch door.

No-one came through it, but the moment was effectively broken. Robert headed past Morgan, back through the house, and bade farewell to the Sullivans with an air of total innocence.

The rush that had accompanied his sudden move toward Morgan, and the feeling of dizziness that came when he had felt her kiss him back, followed Robert at least half-way home.

But no further.

Because as his heart started to slow once more, he found himself thinking that Morgan had better not assume he was going to hang about like a lovesick schoolboy – or worse, try to pursue her. He also hoped that she did not feel the need to confess their moment to her fiancé, who would be able to make life very difficult for Robert.

Though if this was the way Morgan behaved around Robert, presumably this Geoff fellow was also taking a free and easy approach to his engagement. These high society types often did, Robert knew. Morgan had made it clear she wanted nothing from him besides what he had just given to her.

And why would she want anything from him? What was there to want that he could give?

And then, as so often before, Joanna entered his thoughts and refused to leave them.

***

When the last of Morgan's elder brothers had married and left home, her parents had sat her down for a talk. She was the only child of the house now, they told her, and they wanted to be sure she did not become too used to getting her own way.

No-one likes a spoiled wife, her mother had joked – or Morgan had hoped it was a joke, anyway, although they had started bringing up the subject of marriage more and more from that point onward.

Morgan had agreed to pay attention and be grateful for her blessings. And she managed it, for the most part. She was grateful for everything from her schooling to her clothes – to the little things, like the fact that her mother arranged for Morgan's favorite fruit, pears, to always be available at their house.

So when Morgan found that she had been missing out on anything, it often took her by surprise.

Like when she had tasted her first local pear, after moving out to Montana. It had been grown and picked at the precise point of ripeness, and had none of the woodiness or anemic flavor that she was used to with the fruit purchased at city markets. She had eaten it with a sense of wonder and known that she would never appreciate a lesser pear again.

And now – well.

Morgan smiled at Geoff as he glanced over at her from the other side of the carriage. He smiled back, briefly, before looking down at the papers he was holding.

And Morgan felt absolutely nothing.

Or maybe she didn't feel *nothing*. But now her feelings for Geoff had been shown to be so very weak, by comparison to that single hurried moment with Robert.

Mr Cole, Morgan corrected herself, *not Robert.* They were not on intimate terms, they were not friends. And despite the efforts she had made to get her family to extend the hand of friendship to those who lived in the town, they would never be able to become friends. There was too great a distance between them.

"Shall I drop you off at Simon and Isobel's place?" asked Geoff, barely looking at Morgan as they reached the outskirts of town. "I'll join you after I'm done at the bank."

"I'll walk over," said Morgan. "I need to stretch my legs."

She glanced down and saw that one of Geoff's hands was free. She reached over and caught it in her own, smiling once more when he looked at her.

He squeezed her hand and then dropped it.

Of course he did. He almost never tried to hold her hand. He had never once tried to kiss her, except for a quick peck on the cheek when she had accepted his proposal.

And that had been enough. Until now.

Morgan's eyes trailed on the gunsmith store as the carriage rumbled past. She could not see inside, but the door was open, and she knew Robert would be in there.

She narrowed her eyes. This was his fault. Him with his ridiculous smiles and lingering looks. She had been perfectly content before he came along.

***

Robert was trying to level out a shelf that had come loose from its bracket when he heard footsteps entering the store.

"Just a second," he said over his shoulder.

"No rush," came the reply, and Robert almost let go of the shelf. He heard Morgan laugh.

By the time he had affixed the shelf safely, she had wandered to the back of the store, and was lightly running her hand along a row of rifles in their stands.

He fought the urge to tell her to be careful – the stands were a little rickety, and prone to falling over – but she read his expression and smirked a little.

"See, it's upsetting when someone goes where they're not supposed to be," she said, and Robert felt a bite in her words.

"Is that what you think I did?" he asked at once.

She looked a little surprised at his directness, but Robert wasn't going to let her act like this was all his doing.

"You'll notice the door's open, Miss Sullivan. There are no counters or cases in your way. There aren't even any *boundary stones*." Robert raised an eyebrow. "So you're perfectly entitled to be where you are. If I told you to leave and you didn't, then we'd have a problem."

"You shouldn't have kissed me," said Morgan, her fingers tapping lightly against the stock of one of the rifles.

Robert looked her over. She was dressed to go calling, no doubt with one of the *acceptable* families in town, as few of those as there were. The spring green dress warmed her pale skin and brought out a red tint in the coils of her hair.

"Now you tell me," said Robert.

"That's right, I forgot. You don't apologize," said Morgan, rolling her eyes a little.

"Only when I've done something wrong," said Robert. "And if you'd given me any reason to think I had, I would apologize at once."

Morgan flushed.

"You think it's all right to come to someone's house, as a guest, and steal moments with their daughter in the shadows?"

"So you think I wronged your *parents*? Shall I go and apologize to them?" asked Robert. "And are you going to apologize to your fiancé?"

"Don't be stupid."

A step outside on the wooden sidewalk drew their attention, and Robert was suddenly brought back to the night of the party. He wondered what would have happened if he and Morgan had been left alone for longer, just to talk –

No, that was absurd. There was nothing for them to talk about. Nothing could happen between them. He could drop down onto his knees for her and she would laugh him off.

Of course she would. He should be laughing himself, at the very idea of it.

Why wasn't he laughing?

"I didn't steal anything," he told Morgan, dragging her attention back from the fear of being discovered.

Morgan's hand dropped away from the rifles, falling to her side. She clenched both her fists for a moment, and looked as though she was taking a deep breath.

"Oh yes you did," she said, her eyes bright and angry. "And I'm stealing it back."

Robert had no time to think before she had crossed over to him, reached both hands around his shoulders and pulled him down into another kiss.

This one lasted longer than the first.

"What are you doing – " he started to ask after a few moments, but Morgan wouldn't let him break away.

When the kiss eventually ended, Robert took a step backwards, feeling as though he should gasp for air.

Morgan was still staring at him. The color of her face was heightened, her always-cool expression finally looking like something real.

"And who should I apologize to for that?" Robert said, his voice rasping slightly.

She pressed a hand to the side of her face and shook her head.

"I should – I should go – " she reached for the handle of the door, but then drew back.

Robert glanced outside, and saw Morgan's fiancé walking down the street. Morgan moved to the side of the door, out of Geoff's sight. Robert huffed a sigh and leaned against the door jamb.

"He won't come in here," he said. "You can wait til he's gone before you leave."

Morgan nodded, her face still bright pink. Robert couldn't quite guess what she was thinking; maybe she was regretting her actions now she saw her fiancé, or maybe she was scared that someone had them through the shop window.

"No-one really comes in here. Not very often, anyway. There's only so many guns people need in a small town like this," he explained, when Morgan glanced at him.

"I've wondered how most of these businesses manage," she said quietly, looking out at the street.

"Most of them do better than me," said Robert. "Although that reminds me of something I wanted to ask you."

"What?" Morgan had her hands at her cheeks again, as though she was trying to cool them.

"That party at your folks' place," said Robert. "That was your idea, wasn't it?"

"Yes."

Robert tilted his head, waiting for her to explain. She sighed before continuing, rolling her eyes again.

"I realized it was ridiculous that I didn't know your name, and that my parents wouldn't have known it either. I thought if we're going to live here, then we should – well, live here. Get to know everyone."

"Nice to know I made a difference," said Robert.

Morgan threw him a look.

"It's very little to do with you, if you must know. My parents always used to warn me about getting airs about the money we had, and I tried to take it to heart – but sometimes I wonder if they're just saying it, and not acting on it." Morgan frowned. "I'd like to see them live out their ideals."

"They still seem like good people," said Robert, thinking of the brief conversations he had shared with them at the party. They had clearly been aware of his lower status, but had not made Robert feel it.

"They are," said Morgan. "Although I never told them that my best friend growing up was the cook's daughter, and that I used to play with children from the wrong side of town."

"Some might say you still do," said Robert.

Morgan seemed to have regained her composure, because she managed to smirk at this comment.

Her knowing smile, however, failed to give Robert any satisfaction, however, and he was actually relieved when she left a few moments later.

He watched her walk down the street, and wondered what she would tell her fiancé when he asked where she had been.

Part of Robert wanted Morgan to turn around and run back. Another part wanted her to keep going and never return.

He turned away and looked over the quiet store, trying not to reimagine the last few minutes in his head.

No, he did not want her to come back. He did not want to keep making little jokes about whatever was between them – because there was something. And there was no way she would ever acknowledge it.

***

Five times.

Morgan had seen Robert five times since she had sought him out at his store.

Three times had been around town, out in the open. Morgan had been unable to make any comments that might arouse suspicion, and had to keep to normal conversation.

Oddly, she found that she rather enjoyed speaking with Robert. He talked about his sister, and his nieces and nephews, and told Morgan funny stories about the folk around town. But as much as Morgan hoped he would look at her the way he had before, he refused.

A few weeks after their last *private* conversation, she saw Robert in Mr Green's general store. Morgan had thought it was fate that they were the only two in there, but Robert had kept talking to Mr Green, even following him into the storeroom to keep the conversation going when he could have been alone with Morgan.

And, finally, she had gone to Robert's store again. But he had come out of the door as she approached and stood on the pavement, keeping her there where everyone could see them. When she realized that he was doing on purpose, Morgan had been tempted to go inside and knock something over, just to force him back in.

But she had left it, deciding that maybe this would be how it had to end. Because it did have to end, of course it did. She couldn't do what she had done again. Even if she wanted to, she couldn't bring herself to keep betraying Geoff in such a heartless way.

Having decided this, however, she still found herself thinking of Robert – well, any time she wasn't thinking of anything else.

On the afternoon that Robert had refused to speak with her in Mr Green's store, Mr Green had actually kept talking about Robert after he had left. Morgan had stayed quiet and listened, hardly daring to believe her luck, and eagerly drinking in all the details.

Not that it mattered, she reminded herself, that Mr Green thought Robert was one of the best friends he had ever had, or that Robert was a hard worker, or that he sent half his money back to his sister in the east.

It didn't matter, because Robert wasn't hers. And she wasn't his, and that was all there was to it.

And yet again – *again* – she found herself heading to his store the next time she was in town. She waited until she saw someone going in ahead of her, so Robert would have to stay inside, and then headed in herself.

She recognized the man at the counter, and offered a pleasant greeting as Robert stared at her from behind his customer's shoulder.

"My mother was thinking about buying my father a pistol as a gift," she said in explanation, gesturing to one of the only fancy-looking guns in the store. "Don't mention that you saw me in here, all right?"

"Your secret's safe with me," chuckled the man as he left.

Robert did not look pleased to find himself alone with Morgan, and started for the door. She moved to block his path, and he looked down at her in annoyance.

"What was that about being where you don't belong?" he said.

"What about it?" she said.

She had not intended to come in here. She certainly did not have any plans in place, having got Robert alone. But now she was close to him again, Morgan felt her thoughts tumbling into nonsense once more, and looked up as though she was daring Robert to kiss her again.

"I can't do this," he said.

It took a moment for the words to make it into Morgan's mind. When they did, she frowned.

"What do you mean?"

"I can't keep doing this."

Up close, Morgan could see something shadowy in his expression.

"I never asked you to – "

"You'd never have to ask. You know that. You'd just have to stand there for long enough."

"Oh, really?" smiled Morgan.

Robert almost smiled back, but looked away instead.

"Please, Morgan."

Morgan wondered whether that was the first time he had used her first name.

"Please what?"

"Morgan." Robert closed his eyes for a moment when she refused to move. "I know you're just – I don't know, having fun before you settle down – and that's your business – but I can't."

Morgan immediately wanted to defend herself as she heard her actions stated so bluntly.

But what could she have said? That she had real feelings for him, that she would leave Geoff for him? He couldn't be expecting that.

"Don't pretend it wasn't fun for you as well," she said. "Am I supposed to believe you've never kissed anyone before?"

"Not since I was engaged," said Robert.

Mogan finally took a step back.

"When were you engaged?"

"When I first came out here," said Robert, looking relieved to see some space between them. "I'd known her when we were children, and we got engaged when we were eighteen. I was supposed to come out and work, and save up so she could join me."

Robert had leaned back against the counter, his eyes on Morgan's, a direct gaze meant to hold her at a distance.

"What happened?" asked Morgan.

"My sister's husband died," said Robert. "I started sending her money, and I couldn't save up anything for myself. We had to keep waiting, and waiting, and after two and a half years, Joanna had had enough. She wrote to say she was marrying someone else."

"When was this?" asked Morgan, hoping it wasn't too recent.

"Three years back." Robert shrugged, his expression becoming wry. "It was just as well, as I think I wouldn't have been able to save up enough even now. She'd still be waiting."

"But you have a place to live, you have a business, and friends," said Morgan, her thoughts heating at the injustice. "She could have married you as you are now."

Robert smiled his lopsided half-smile.

"Would you?" he asked.

And there it was.

Robert kept looking at Morgan as all her remaining thoughts and words fell away.

She could not pretend. There was nothing to pretend. This was why she was here, because she cared for him, and she knew he cared for her, and she wouldn't let him do anything about it.

If there had been any hope in Robert's question, he had it well hidden, because his expression did not fall as Morgan remained silent.

"I have to thank you," he said after a moment. "I finally realized that I'd only been hanging around here for so long because I didn't want to admit I'd failed."

"What do you mean?" asked Morgan, feeling a sudden dread.

"I'm going to go home. Spend some time with my sister and her kids. Mr Green has a cousin who's interested in buying the business." Robert looked around the store. "It'll be easier to support my sister if I'm close. And I'm not afraid of going back and seeing Joanna. Not any more."

There was the half-smile again, and then Robert was walking over to the door of the store. He was waiting for her to leave.

Morgan trailed after him, feeling dizzy.

"But – but won't you – " *kiss me, stay with me, don't go, don't go, don't go,* " – say goodbye, at least?"

They were standing on the sidewalk, and Morgan almost kissed him right there, not caring who saw. But he kept the distance between them.

He had stopped smiling.

"I would have fought for you," he said. "I would have loved you if you'd let me."

He did not wait for a reply before walking back into the store.

***

Robert looked up as he walked through the park, eyeing the clouds above. In Lawson, the rain would have started falling already, but here it was holding back, like it wasn't sure whether it would be appreciated.

The city his sister lived in wasn't that big, but after five years in a town with two roads, Robert sometimes felt a little overwhelmed. He enjoyed walking home through the park, which was the quietest spot he could find.

Some days, he missed his old town, and the wide open spaces that came with it. But most days he had his sister's kids to spend time with, and his new business to work on, and friends to make.

And today, he could remind himself that if he was still in Lawson, he would have had to hear everyone talking about Morgan's wedding to Geoff.

It felt absurd that he remembered the date. He did not even know who had told it to him.

Robert paused by a bench overlooking a patch of grass on which a few children were playing, and sat down. He could see the city clocktower through a gap in the trees, and tried not to think about the fact that the ceremony would be over by now. Morgan would be married.

"You're terribly hard to find, did you know that?"

Robert turned towards the voice that came from the path next to the bench. Then he had to stare for several seconds before he could understand what he was seeing.

"Morgan?"

That couldn't be her. It couldn't be.

"I stopped by your house, and your sister thought you'd be at work, but they said you'd already left. I had to use all my tracking skills."

Morgan walked over to the bench, halting for a moment in front of Robert, who was so stunned he didn't even think to stand. She looked as though she were not entirely real, standing out against the park's greens and grays in a bright blue coat, the color of a hot summer sky.

"Mr Green gave me your address, in case you were wondering," she said. "He sends his best."

"Aren't you meant to be getting married?" Robert said, unwilling to move for the fear that she might disappear before his eyes.

"Married?" Morgan frowned. "Is today the twelfth? I lost track of the days on the train."

"You're not – "

"I'm not married, no," said Morgan, apparently deciding that Robert was not going to move, and sitting beside him on the bench.

"And you're here."

"Well, I *think* I'm here," said Morgan. "Does it look like I'm someplace else?"

This finally broke through Robert's stunned thoughts, and he laughed.

"What are you doing here, then?" he asked.

"I was going to write," Morgan said, "but I wanted to apologize in person."

Robert squinted at her. "I keep telling you, you only need to apologize when you do something wrong."

Did she mean that she was here to see him? That couldn't be right.

"But I did do something wrong," said Morgan. "I let you believe I was just – what did you call it? Having fun." When she repeated the words, Robert saw her wince slightly.

"I'm sorry – " he began.

"Excuse me," said Morgan, holding up her hand. "This is my apology. Get your own."

Robert could not laugh again, now that his heart had started to pound so hard it was hurting. The way she was looking at him was making it hard to breathe.

"I was angry at you for making me feel the way I did," said Morgan. "I wanted you to prove that you were only playing, so I could pretend I was as well."

"But you weren't?" asked Robert.

"Not even a little." Morgan smiled. "And I've loved you more than anything."

A breath forced its way into Robert's lungs.

Morgan leaned over and pressed her lips to his cheek. Robert's eyes dipped closed for a second, the moment meaning so much more than their previous kisses of hunger and desperation.

He reached out and took Morgan's hand, grinning when she blushed as though it was the first time they had ever touched.

She was here for him. She had come here, all the way out here, just for him, to tell him this.

"And I've loved you," he said. "Even when I thought you wouldn't let me."

Morgan smiled. Robert caught a glance thrown from a man walking past them, across the grass. He nodded a little, just a small acknowledgement of their happiness. *We must look like a normal couple,* Robert thought. Normal and happy.

"Do your parents know you're here?" he asked suddenly.

"They do." Morgan glanced at him. "There was some... loud discussion, when I left, but they'll come around."

"You're sure?" Robert could only imagine what they must think of him right now.

"All my brothers made good marriages, so they were due at least marital *contretemps.* Or that's what I told them, anyway," Morgan said. "They've nothing to complain about."

Morgan looked cheerfully optimistic, but Robert felt doubtful.

"I should write to them," he said.

"That's probably a good idea."

"Oh, and – what about Geoff?" This was another unpleasant thought, but not one that could be postponed. Robert had never imagined being the type of man who could steal someone else's fiancée.

For the first time, Morgan looked genuinely regretful.

"You told him?" asked Robert. "He ended things?"

"I did tell him. But I was already going to end things, dear." Morgan shook her head. "Even if you turned me away, I couldn't think of marrying him, after everything. He still wanted to, you know."

"He did?"

"He said he would forgive me," said Morgan, "though I had my doubts. Regardless, I managed to convince him he deserved better than me."

"You're probably right."

Morgan pouted in pretend-offense, then laughed.

"I think we probably deserve each other," she said.

"Well don't say *that*," grinned Robert. "But just so you know, I really am – "

This time, Morgan placed her hand against his mouth, just for a moment, to stop him finishing the sentence.

"I meant it," she said. "No more apologies. Not til you've done something wrong."

"What about stealing you?" Robert asked.

Morgan squeezed his hand.

"You can't steal me," she said. "I'm already yours."

TELL IT TO MY HEART

24

Chapter One

Mandy Hostetler took a deep breath and let it out slowly. Raising the bat to her shoulder, she narrowed her eyes and watched the ball carefully as Sam released it from his grasp and sent it sailing through the air. Mandy lifted the bat and gave it a fast swing, her heart beating fast as she heard the wood make contact with the hard, leather ball.

"Look at it go!" One of the boys yelled as the ball went flying up over the trees and into a nearby field.

Mandy lowered the bat to her side and smiled triumphantly.

"Good job, Mandy!" Levi exclaimed.

Mandy threw her head back and laughed as the twelve-year-old boy gave a little dance. "Mandy!" In the distance, she could hear her mother calling to her from their large, two-story white house, "Mandy *kumm*!"

With a deep sigh, Mandy handed Levi the ball bat and slowly shook her head, "Sounds like *mamm* needs me for something."

Making the short trip to the back door of the Hostetler home, Mandy passed several Amish men who were standing in the front yard enjoying their time together after the church service.

Stepping in the kitchen, Mandy immediately found her mother standing at the kitchen sink washing a pile of dishes.

"*Ach*, child, where have you been?" Mrs. Hostetler exclaimed, giving Mandy a look of semi-disgust.

Reaching down to knock some dried mud off the bottom of her dress, Mandy laughed and braced herself for a sharp reproof from her mother, "Oh, the boys wanted me to play some softball with them. I didn't intend to be gone for long."

Glancing at the group of Amish women buzzing around in the kitchen, Mrs. Hostetler lowered her voice and whispered, "Can't you behave yourself like a lady at least on Sunday?"

Suzie Christner reached out to grab a clean dish, wiping it with a dish towel, "Mandy, when are you going to drop the wooden ball bat long enough to grab onto a boyfriend?"

Mandy smirked as she washed her hands in the wash basin and then started to put away a pile of dried plates, "Of all the things I need, a boyfriend is not one of them!" She declared, "I'm twenty-five-years-old and I've been fine without one this long….I don't see why that would change."

Lizzie Eicher said, "Oh, Mandy, you don't know what you're missing out on! A man is *gut* for so much. I know you've caught plenty of attention too! If the men aren't won over by your looks, they certain are interested once they taste your cooking!"

Mandy shook her head, "I'm good with a hammer and I can break a horse. I can spend my day out in the fields and then come in at night to cook my own supper." Giving a shrug, she announced, "There's nothing a man can do that I can't. So why would I need one?"

Hoisting her chubby baby up on her hip, Lizzie tossed in, "You can't have a family on your own."

Mandy narrowed her eyes and shook her head, "That's fine…because children are another thing I simply don't want!"

The group of women all laughed – all, that is, but Mandy's mother. Mrs. Hostetler muttered, "I had hoped that sending her to stay with her grandmother during the week would help calm her down some. But, since I sent her, she's spent her time not only reading Granny books and cooking her meals…but has also been up on the roof patching the shingles."

Although Mandy could tell her mother was disgusted, her announcement brought another round of laugher from the women.

Mandy smiled to herself. Let her *mamm* fret and fuss as much as she wanted. Mandy wouldn't be getting married. Ever!

Each Sunday night, Mandy would hitch up the buggy and travel the short two-mile trip to her granny's house where she would stay until Friday afternoon. While Mandy's granny was strong and healthy, she was nearing her ninety-sixth birthday and needed a lot of help around her house.

When Mandy entered her granny's house that Sunday afternoon, Granny was sitting in her rocking chair, a quilt thrown across her knees and her Bible spread across her lap.

"*Gut* evening, Granny!" Mandy exclaimed as she hurried to hang up her shawl, "Have you had anything to eat?"

Granny shook her head, "I just started one of your delicious cinnamon rolls." She motioned toward a sticky sweet treat on a plate beside her, "That's plenty for me."

Mandy smiled, "I'm glad you like them."

"Child, your cooking is better than that of anyone else!" Granny exclaimed, reaching up to readjust her glasses, "I've heard people in the community brag on your treats."

Mandy let out a sigh as she sat down in another chair opposite her grandmother, "Ugh, I've heard plenty about that today. All the women kept teasing me about catching a husband with my cooking."

Granny laughed and then shook her head, "*Ach*, child, things never change! As long as I can remember, the married women aren't happy as long as an unmarried woman is in the community. A bunch of matchmakers, they are!"

Mandy jutted out her bottom jaw, "Well, they're just going to have to learn to be happy now, because I'm *not* getting married!"

"Ah, sweet child," Granny smiled as she reached out and patted a weathered hand on top of Mandy's, "What will you do if the Lord has a man in store for you?"

Mandy shook her head stubbornly, "I'm pretty much certain the Lord has nothing like that planned for me. There are no men who have ever caught my attention. I'd be a bad wife to anyone."

Granny chucked and sighed as she looked down at her Bible, "As you say, dear, as you say."

Mandy wasn't enjoying Granny's conversation. She could handle a lot of things, but she didn't appreciate it when Granny started bringing

God into these discussions. Quickly excusing herself, she hurried upstairs to get ready for bed.

Chapter Two

Monday morning found Mandy on top of the kitchen roof with a nail gripped between her teeth and a shingle in her hands. The hot August sun beat down on her head, causing her to reach up and wipe sweat from her brow.

The sound of a vehicle pulling into the driveway caused Mandy to sit up straight and become alert. A shiny blue Ford truck stopped in front of the house. Through the tinted windows, Mandy couldn't make out the driver.

"Hello!" Mandy called down when the driver's door opened. A strange man stepped out. Dressed in a button-up shirt and khaki pants, he seemed oddly out of place.

Glancing up at the roof, he nodded in her direction and called out, "Is this the home of Anne Hostetler?"

"Wait just a minute!" Mandy replied as she scampered across the roof and to the ladder that was leaned against the side of the house.

When she reached the ground, Mandy wiped her hands across her dress and worked to tuck her hair back under her prayer cap.

"Is Mrs. Hostetler home?" The stranger asked.

Mandy viewed him in suspicion, "Who are you?"

"Dr. Matt Byler," he threw out a hand in Mandy's direction, "The last time Mrs. Hostetler was at the hospital, the doctors had some concerns and asked me to come out to check on her."

Something about the stranger unnerved Mandy. He didn't have a particularly bad feeling to him, but he made her uncomfortable. His brown eyes were too solemn and, as she took his hand in her own, something about the feel of his smooth skin felt unfamiliar and strange. He certainly wasn't like the men she was used to within the Amish community.

"She's inside," Mandy managed to mumble, "Come on in."

Leading Dr. Matt into the house, Mandy directed him to the sitting room where Granny was napping in her rocking chair.

"Granny," she spoke up, "Someone is here to see you!"

Opening her eyes, Granny sat up in surprise.

"Hi there," Dr. Matt said with a smile as he squatted down beside her chair, "I'm Dr. Matt Byler. The hospital suggested that I stop by and see how you are doing. I hear you had some problems with your heart a few weeks ago."

As Dr. Matt talked more about Granny's recent health scare that turned out to be nothing serious, Mandy went to the kitchen to bring out some of her fresh apple pie. Dishing it out onto a plate, Mandy wondered if this *Englischer* had ever tasted anything quite like her pie. Just the thought of it brought a haughty smile to Mandy's face.

Stepping into the sitting room, Mandy listened as Dr. Matt looked Granny over and announced, "I hope I'm in as good shape when I'm sixty as you are at ninety-five."

Rising to his feet, Dr. Matt turned and sat down in the other rocking chair, "Your bouts of breathlessness do worry me. I would like to keep a close eye on this and possibly hook you up to a heart monitor so we can make sure that your heart is functioning properly."

"Here," Mandy took the opportunity to pass him a plate of pie, "Have some apple pie."

"No, thank you," Dr. Matt returned with a shrug, "I don't like apple pie."

Raising an eyebrow, Mandy said, "Perhaps that's because you've never had *my* apple pie."

The doctor opened his mouth to protest but then reached out to take the plate in his hand.

"How long have you been practicing medicine?" Granny asked.

Dr. Matt took a bite of the pie and swallowed, "I graduated last year. I used to live in this area and decided to move back to start my practice. Once I get established, I plan to quit working with the hospital and start a small clinic nearby."

"Do you make house calls often?"

Dr. Matt set his plate aside, the rest of his pie untouched, "I would like to work closely with the Amish community and I know that house calls would be beneficial, so yes, I plan to ultimately offer house visits on a regular basis."

Granny clapped her hands together in surprise and smiled, "*Ach*, how wonderful that will be! We have such a time trying to find drivers to take us places and driving to the doctor on a buggy can be such a difficult experience. You will be the answer to our prayers!"

Dr. Matt looked down at his hands and finally said, "Well, I suppose I should move on. I'll be needed back at the hospital soon." Pulling himself to his feet, he let Mandy lead him to the front door. Reaching in his pocket, the doctor pulled out a business card, "Here. This has all my contact information. If you need me, let me know and I'll be over as quickly as possible."

Dr. Matt then handed Mandy the plate full of pie. Giving a smirk, he announced softly, "No matter how good of a cook you *think* you are, I still don't like apples."

Mandy stood speechless, the plate of hardly-touched pie in one hand and his business card in the other.

"Goodbye, Mrs. Hostetler!" He called out as he opened the front door, "I'll be back in the next few days with your test results."

"*Danki* for the visit!" She returned.

"You're welcome."

As the doctor drove away, Mandy found herself faced with a mixture of different emotions. How dare he insult her by not eating her pie! Her pie was famous as being the best in the community; *Englischers* usually couldn't get enough. But, on the other hand, Mandy felt more curious about him than any other man she had ever met.

Shaking her head, Mandy tried to clear away the thoughts that were assailing her. *Ach*, she had no interest in *any* man – let alone an *Englischer*!

Chapter Three

Despite the fact that Mandy had been shaken by Dr. Matt's lack of interest in her pie, she quickly put it out of her mind. Life around Granny's house was too busy to be fretting about the opinion of a rude *Englischer*. Mandy busied herself keeping up with the laundry, baking some goods for a local Amish store, and designing a plan for the new chicken coop she was going to build.

No, Mandy didn't have time to think about the handsome young doctor and had put him entirely out of her mind until she saw his truck pull into view Thursday afternoon.

Grimacing to herself, Mandy pulled a pie out of the oven, wishing for all she was worth that she could throw it right in his face.

"Hello," Dr. Matt called out as he knocked on the front door. Mandy hurried to open it, a scowl on her face.

"Granny," she called out, "That doctor is here to see you again!"

"Oh, *gut*!" Granny replied, pulling herself up from the kitchen table where she had been busy breaking beans, "It's *wunderbar-gut* to see you again, doctor!"

"It's wonderful good to see you, too." The doctor replied with a smile.

Mandy went back to the stove, giving him a side-wise glance of surprise when she realized that he understood her grandmother's Amish language.

"You're full of surprises, doctor!" Granny exclaimed, "How do you know Amish?"

The doctor smiled and laid a folder on the table with a shrug, "I grew up around Amish as a boy. I know the language and a lot of the customs." Opening a folder, he announced, "All of your tests came back in good shape. It seems you have no serious health concerns."

Mandy let out a sigh of relief as she hurried to spread soft homemade icing on a plate of fresh cookies.

"As far as it goes, I just advise you to keep doing what you're doing." Dr. Matt replied, "Whatever you're doing, it must be right."

Granny chuckled, "Well, I get by with a lot of prayer and a lot of my granddaughter's cookies. Would you like one, doctor?"

Mandy instantly felt her defenses go up, "I'm sure he doesn't want one, Granny..."

"No," Dr. Matt replied, "I like cookies. Besides, if they'll help me stay as health as your grandmother, I think eating one is a good choice."

Passing him the plate, Mandy found herself holding her breath, hoping he wouldn't reject this treat like he had her pie.

"Are you enjoying your time in this area?" Granny asked.

"Oh, yeah," Dr. Matt answered around a bite of cookie, "I couldn't be happier. I have met so many great people. The Amish are keeping me busy since I make house calls, and I still have my work at the hospital as well."

Wiping some crumbs off his pants, Mandy was relieved to hear him say, "That was a very good cookie." Standing up, he glanced over at the plates of treats on the counter and exclaimed, "I hope you don't plan to eat all of these!"

Mandy had to laugh at his comment and quickly explained, "I'm supposed to take them into town to a little Amish store. Speaking of which, I need to go call a driver to take me into town. I have a way back, but not a way there." Although she hated to ask, Mandy managed to force out the question, "Is there any chance I could borrow your phone?"

Dr. Matt smiled, "I can do even better than that. I'm headed to the hospital, so I can take you into town myself."

The idea of being alone with the good-looking *Englischer* suddenly made Mandy feel uncomfortable. Shifting from one foot to the other, she searched her mind for any excuse to say no.

"What a good idea!" Granny threw in, "Mandy, this will work out so *gut* for you!"

Mandy slowly nodded her head, "*Ach*, all right, that would be good. Thank you."

The trip to the store felt uncomfortable with Mandy positioned in the front of the truck next to the doctor.

"Have you ever driven a truck before?" Dr. Matt asked, obviously looking for anything to start conversation.

Mandy laughed and shook her head, "Oh, no, that's not the Amish way! But I certainly have wanted to at times."

The doctor shook his head, a sadness suddenly evident in his dark eyes, "It's not so great. Between you and me, I think you've got it better. I'd much rather be riding behind a buggy than maneuvering the *Englischer* world."

His words caused Mandy to laugh again. Over the years, she had often wished that she wasn't so confined by her faith. The idea of breaking free to encounter everything the world had to offer was intoxicating. Although she had given up her wild ideas and chosen to stay within the Amish community, she still had to be somewhat envious of anyone with a truck.

"How old are you?" He asked bluntly.

"Twenty-five. How about you?"

Dr. Matt laughed, "I'm thirty." Thinking for a moment, he announced, "You're mighty bold for an Amish woman. Is that why you're not married?"

Mandy felt her face grow warm and she jutted out her bottom jaw, "I'm not married because I choose not to be married. Believe me, I've had plenty of opportunities. What about you? Thirty is certainly old not to be married. Are you too rude to get married? Or have you been married and she left you?"

The doctor threw his head back and laughed this time, "Oh, wow, your gentle way of saying things makes me feel so good. No, I've not been married…and I have no intentions of ever being married. I decided a long time ago that marriage isn't for me. I haven't had a girlfriend in about ten years now."

Mandy was silent for a moment, suddenly realizing that she and this strange *Englischer* had something in common. While this realization made her disturbed, it also brought a strange wave of comfort.

Pointing to the Amish store on the right, Mandy showed Dr. Matt where she needed to get out. Surprisingly enough, she found herself wishing that their ride had lasted a little longer.

Chapter Four

Once again, Mandy spent the weekend with her family, trying her best to keep from saying anything that would cause her *mamm* to scold her. By the time Sunday night came, Mandy was ready to get back to Granny's house. She almost wished that she could stay with Granny every day and completely cut out her visits back home.

Taking a deep breath, she unhitched her buggy out in the barn and then made her way to Granny's house. Evening was quickly closing in and Mandy wanted a few minutes to unwind before heading off to bed.

Opening the front door, she called out, "Granny, I'm home!"

"Mandy…" A weak voice called out, "Mandy…help me."

Suddenly frightened, Mandy hurried into the sitting room where she found her Granny lying flat on her side in the overturned rocking chair. Her head was bleeding and her eyes looked lifeless.

"Granny, oh, Granny!" Mandy fell to her knees and reached out, unsure of what to do next.

"Get…help…" Granny whispered.

Pulling herself to her feet, Mandy was unsure who she should call. Running to the table, she found Dr. Matt's phone number and hurried out to the phone shanty at the edge of the lane.

Dr. Matt was at the house within ten minutes. Mandy watched as he jumped out of his shiny truck and race toward the front door.

"She's in here," Mandy announced, directing him to the sitting room where Granny still lay in a heap on the floor, "I was afraid to move her."

Dr. Matt squatted down on the floor, "Mrs. Hostetler, where are you hurt?" Reaching out, he felt for broken bones.

"Nothing seems to be broken," he informed Mandy, "Can you help me move her to her bed?"

With a moan from Granny, the doctor scooped her up in his arms like a newborn child, following Mandy as she led him to the bedroom.

Watching him lay Granny down on the bed, Mandy was hit by the realization that, on her own, there was no way she could have moved her grandmother.

"Get her a glass of water," Dr. Matt instructed and Mandy hurried to do as he asked.

"Can you tell us what happened?" The doctor questioned.

After taking a drink of water, Granny whispered, "*Ach*, it happened so suddenly! I was sitting in my chair asleep, and the crazy thing turned right over. Next thing I knew, I was on the floor and I couldn't get up."

"How long were you lying there?"

"Well, let's see..." She tried to think, "I fell right after Mandy left Friday night."

"You've been on the floor with no food or water for this long?" Letting out a whistle, the doctor exclaimed, "I'm surprised you're still alive."

Taking a deep breath, Granny whispered, "I suppose the *gut* Lord isn't done with me yet."

Turning to Mandy, Dr. Matt announced, "We need to get her to the hospital. I'll call an ambulance."

"No...no hospital!" Granny exclaimed, trying to raise her feeble voice, "I want to stay right here."

Glancing at Mandy, Dr. Matt searched her face for an opinion. Mandy shrugged her shoulders and whispered, "She's always hated hospitals. She's said she'd rather die at home than have to stay at one of those places."

Dr. Matt started to protest but then slowly nodded his head, "I can see how she would feel that way. If I lived here, I would want to be home, too."

Raising his voice, he announced, "All right, but I'll have to stay here with you. I'm not leaving you alone until I see that you're going to be okay. I'll run by my office and get some supplies so that I can stitch up that place on your forehead and get some IV fluids going."

"*Danki*," Mandy whispered softly, "*Danki* so much."

Within the next hour, Dr. Matt had the gash in Granny's head stitched up and fluids going into her body thanks to an IV. He sat by the old woman's side until she finally fell asleep.

Watching him carefully, Mandy could see that he was exhausted as well. He reached up to rub his eyes and yawn.

"Would you like to lay down somewhere and take a nap?" Mandy questioned.

The doctor shook his head slowly, "I don't want to sleep until I makes sure she's going to be okay."

"Would you like some coffee?"

Dr. Matt nodded, "Coffee would be nice."

Following her into the kitchen, the doctor sat down in one of the wooden chairs and let out a deep breath. Reaching up to rub his eyes, he whispered, "Wake me when the coffee's finished."

Mandy busied herself preparing the hot drink. Turning around with a cup in hand, she found the doctor with his head resting against the table top, sound asleep. He looked so sweet, so childlike, that Mandy felt a strange tugging at her heart – a feeling she'd never experienced before.

"Dr..." Mandy placed the cup in front of him and placed a gentle hand on his shoulder, "Doctor...your coffee is ready."

Sitting up straight and rubbing his eyes, the doctor exclaimed, "Wow, sorry...how long have I been asleep?"

"About ten minutes," Mandy replied with a laugh, "Here," she indicated to his cup and then passed him a cinnamon roll, "Do you have anything against cinnamon rolls?"

He smirked and shook his head, "No, I actually like those a lot, too. Apple is really the only thing I don't like...and yours wasn't that bad, really....I just wanted to irritate you."

Mandy couldn't decide if she'd rather slap him or hug him for that admission.

"Doctor..."

"Please," he held up his hand as he took a sip of his coffee, "Don't call me doctor anymore. Matt or Matthew is fine."

Mandy sat back in her seat and slowly nodded her head, "All right, Matt."

Taking a bite of her cinnamon roll, Matt closed his eyes and whispered, "This tastes just like my *mamm's*."

The words took Mandy by surprise. Sitting up straighter, she exclaimed, "What did you just say?"

Matt smirked and swallowed, "Well, that slipped out...but it was almost worth it to see your face." Wiping his mouth on a napkin, he confessed, "I haven't always lived in the *English* world."

Mandy could feel her eyes growing as large as saucers, "You left?"

"Technically no...more like was kidnapped." Matt sighed, "When I was twelve, my *mamm* died. My dad went a little crazy after that. There were three of us kids and he packed us all up and moved us to the city. He was done being Amish, he said. Within a few months, he was a heavy alcoholic and moved us in with a girlfriend who liked my two sisters, but could hardly stand me." Shaking his head, Matt said, "The *Englisch* world was nothing like life in the Amish community."

"*Ach*," Mandy closed her eyes and leaned her forehead against the palm of her hand, "What happened?"

Matt shrugged, "What you see now. I made it my mission in life to become a doctor so that I could help people like my mom. My dad drank himself to death. My sisters fell right into the *Englischer* world and are now married, successful business women. They forgot everything about this world...but I never could."

"You miss being Amish, don't you?"

Matt slowly nodded, "Every day, I've wished that I could just be back home...but there's no way now."

"Why not?"

Matt shook his head, "I'm not good Amish material. I can't see myself farming with a happy wife and a dozen kids. Really, Mandy, can you see that?"

Mandy sighed deeply and tried to picture any of the Amish women she knew being happy with someone like Matt.

"I'd better go check on your grandma," he announced, scooting his cup back, "*Danki* for the food."

Chapter Five

With each day that passed, Granny slowly improved. By Wednesday, Matt felt safe leaving to go back to his work at the hospital and regular house calls among the Amish community. While Mandy was glad that her grandmother was doing better, it made her sad to see Matt gone.

During Matt's stay, Mandy had begun to enjoy his company. Unlike the other Amish men she had known, he wasn't desperate for her attention and wasn't trying to make her become his wife. They had enjoyed quality time together, sharing stories of their experiences growing up in the Amish community.

Matt slowly explained sadder details about his time in the *Englischer* world. He told Mandy how confusing it had been to start public school along with the bullies that he had encountered. It was obvious that Matt had never fit in the regular world and now he seemed convinced that he could never fit in the Amish world either.

Mandy felt her heart softening so much. As much as she hated to admit it, she felt love growing for this handsome young doctor. She wanted to tell Matt how she felt, she wanted to let him know that she would welcome him into their community, but her pride kept her from opening her mouth. *Ach*, she had spent her entire life vowing that she would never care about a man! The idea of admitting she had been wrong was more than she could do.

By the next week, Granny was able to get up and move around with very little pain. She was off of the IV fluids and was able to eat and drink whatever she wanted.

Thursday afternoon, Matt stopped by for his daily visit. Although Mandy tried to hide her excitement, she felt a thrill in her heart.

"You certainly do look better now!" Matt announced as he looked over Granny, "Mrs. Hostetler, you are one tough lady!"

Although his words sounded happy, his voice seemed sad. Mandy instantly detected that he was unhappy about something.

"I've got some surprising news..." Matt said, looking down at the top of his shoes, "I got an offer to go to Boston to work in a really great hospital. I had a hard time deciding, but I'm going to accept."

Mandy felt like the wind had been knocked right out of her chest. Staggering, she held onto the wall for support.

"*Ach*, why?" Granny asked, "I thought you were happy here."

Matt gave a shrug, "Sometimes happiness is a double-edged sword. I need to leave."

Standing to his feet, he closed his medical bag, "I'm going to give my patients over to one of my associates at the hospital. Doctor Brown....you'll like him."

Mandy felt herself blinking furiously, trying to hold back her tears.

"It was nice to meet you, Mrs. Hostetler. It was *gut* to meet you too, Mandy."

And like that, he was gone. Mandy followed him to the front door, but she couldn't force words to come out of her mouth.

"I can't believe it," Mandy whispered, trying to gather her emotions, "I can't believe he's leaving."

"Why didn't you stop him?!" Granny exclaimed, throwing her hands up in surprise and irritation.

"How could I stop him?" Mandy retorted, "He's determined to go."

Granny reached out and placed her weathered hand on Mandy's shoulder, "Tell him how you feel! Dear girl, can't you see...this is the man for you!"

Mandy ripped away from her, her face growing hot with embarrassment, "I don't know what you're talking about."

"You love him! I can see it in your face every time he's here!"

Mandy jutted out her bottom jaw defiantly, "I will *never* love a man!" And with that, she stormed out of the room and to her bedroom.

Mandy couldn't sleep that night. She kept turning from side to side, her mind full of thoughts about Matt. Granny was right: She did love him. Mandy knew that it was true. The question was, was her love bigger than her pride? She didn't think it could be. No matter how much Matt wanted to be a part of her world or how much she enjoyed being around him, she knew that she would sooner die than have to admit that everyone was right and that she could need another person.

The next day, Mandy tried to work on driving posts for the chicken coop, but her mind was so full of frustration that she could do nothing right. She hit her thumb twice and dropped the fence post on her foot.

"That's it!" She finally exclaimed as she threw the fence post to the ground in disgust, "I've got to go to him!"

Despite never needing a man in the past, Mandy realized that she truly did need one now. She needed Matt...and she wanted him.

Now that she had made her decision, she could hardly wait. She hurried out to the barn and hitched up the wagon. Running into the house, she told Granny she had to go into town.

"Where are you going, child?" Granny exclaimed, rousing from her rocking chair.

"To see Matt!" Mandy announced, grabbing for her shawl, "You're right Granny. I've got to talk to him."

In all the times that she had raced her buggy, Mandy had never gone any faster. By the time she reached town, sweat was pouring down her face. Remembering where Matt had pointed out his office, she stopped in front of it, breathing a sigh of relief when she saw his truck parked beside it.

"Matt," She called out, slinging the door open.

Matt stood at the desk surrounded by cardboard boxes he was filling with papers from a drawer. When he heard her voice, he looked up in surprise, "Mandy! Is your granny all right?"

Mandy nodded and bent over, trying to catch her breath.

"Matt," Mandy tried to speak around the pounding of her heart, "Oh, Matt, I don't even know how to tell you this. Don't go. Please, I know it's crazy, but don't go. We need you here...I need you here."

Matt seemed to be soaking in her words. He carefully laid a pile of papers in one of the boxes and stood up straight to look her in the eyes.

"A lot of places need me," he replied, "I'm a good doctor...and the hospital in Boston needs a good doctor."

Suddenly, Mandy found her eyes filling with tears that she struggled to contain, "I don't mean that, Matt. I know that you're a fine doctor, but that's not what I need...I need *you*. Matt, I love you."

In an instant, Matt had crossed the distance between them. Gathering Mandy in his arms, he held her tightly against him as she sobbed into his shirt.

"Are you serious?" He asked, pushing her back and propping her chin up so that he could look in her face, "Are you sure that you mean what you're saying?"

Mandy nodded against the tears, so anxious to be back at home in his embrace, "Please, don't leave! I know you want to go to Boston..."

"I don't want to go to Boston," he interrupted, "I don't want to ever leave this place. As soon as I started practicing here, the urge to rejoin the Amish church was greater than ever. And knowing you....Mandy, you've nearly driven me crazy. Every time I was with you, I have wanted so desperately to love you, but I knew that you would never let me. I knew you were so determined to stay single that you wouldn't think of being with me. Leaving was my way of escaping the sadness of knowing we could never be together!"

Mandy shook her head, once again burying her black cap against his chest, "I could never be happy being single now!"

"Neither could I," he agreed, pulling her closer to him.

Together they stood in the office, enjoying their new-found romance, both realizing that to love and be loved were the greatest of all things life had to offer.

Prologue

Mandy reached up to wipe a strand of hair out of her eyes, never taking her gaze off the ball. She held her bat above her shoulder and waited for it. As soon as the ball came her direction, she gave a quick swing of her arm, watching as the wooden bat sent it sailing far across the fields.

"Yay for Mom!!!" The pitcher started yelling.

Mandy laughed as a group of boys, her boys, started gathering around her.

"I'll never be as good as you are, *Mamm*!" One of the boys started to complain.

Mandy laughed and reached up to give his straw hat a playful flip, "Now, now, you've just got to practice. And I have to get inside and finish up on supper before your *daed* gets home from work."

The boys hurried off to finish their chores while Mandy dusted some dirt off her skirt.

"You're a little too late on that one." Matt's voice spoke softly in her ear. Turning around, Mandy realized that he crept up behind her.

Wrapping her arms around his neck, she looked up into his brown eyes. Over the past fifteen years, they had weathered a lot together.

Shortly after they admitted their love for each other, Matt joined the Amish church. Since doctors were so necessary, the Bishop agreed that he could keep his medical practice. Mandy and Matt had gotten married and now had six children of their own.

The two of them lived together with Granny until she passed on, leaving them her house for their own. In Mandy's spare time, she still ran a farm, baked goods, and did small carpentry jobs.

"What are you thinking about?" Matt laughed at Mandy's goofy smile.

Mandy smirked and reached up to give him a kiss, "I was just thinking how glad I am that Granny was right about God having a man in store for me."

Matt smiled back at her. Together, they walked to the house where Mandy finished up on a delicious meal for her family to enjoy together.

BENEATH THE AMISH SKY

NIKKI SALEM

<u>Chapter One</u>

She didn't love him.

She'd never love him.

Anna knew better than to think in absolutes, knew that she shouldn't assume she knew better than her father, but she would never love Samuel. Not if she was given a thousand years, not if he were actually closer to her age.

She was hardly twenty-one.

Hardly out of age for going to Sings and getting to court properly, her Rumspringa wasn't even finished.

Her father thought he knew what was best for her.

Samuel was an absolute nightmare though.

He was almost thirty-five, married once but his wife left to be English.

When Anna had first heard about this she felt terrible for him. It was horrifying to think that someone you pledged your life to could just leave you behind without a second thought. To live a life neither of you were familiar with. Anna couldn't imagine how selfish and cruel his ex-wife must have been. Leaving behind a chance at growing a family, at starting a life together, sounded outrageous-

Until she properly got to know Samuel.

His wife had made the right decision, and as she knew him better Anna began to envy the mystery woman who had flown the coup.

Samuel was boring, uninteresting, repetitive. He worked in the church, which her father found more than respectable, and so all he spoke of was the church. He went on for literal hours about repairs he wanted to do to the meeting building, hardly pausing to breathe. He didn't care to listen to her, or to stop once she was obviously uncomfortable. In all of the hours her parents had let him speak with her, she'd probably spoken less than twenty words.

She didn't want to have to live with that forever.

Anna couldn't imagine another sixty years, or more, of her life dedicated to this man who didn't care about anything but himself and the image the church gave him.

She couldn't see herself ever loving him, so marriage was a horrifying prospect.

The evening sun was just beginning to settle on the edge of the horizon. Her father had made up his mind, and all she could do was hope to dissuade him somehow. Gathering the last of the laundry for the next day, she listened for his tell-tale footsteps.

He was her father, she knew it was sad to be so nervous, but she was.

Sucking in a deep breath, she urged her feet forward, out to the kitchen where he was standing and drinking water.

"Father, may we speak?" she asked, her hands settled in front of her.

"Yes, what is it?" he asked, he was covered in mud from the day's work.

"I can't marry Samuel," she laid the words out neatly between them. Her father's mood seemed to immediately crumple into aggravation.

"You will," he replied back simply.

"Father I don't love him," she said, shaking her head. "He's so boring, I can't imagine a worse match," she admitted, approaching him.

"What does that matter?" her father asked, his voice raising. "You're supposed to be building a home and a family together, you'll love him in the end," he shook his head.

"I won't marry him," she said, standing her ground in a way she never had with her father.

"Are you saying my decisions aren't good enough for you?" he asked, slamming his hat down on the table.

"No, I-"

"You are my daughter, you had your chance to choose, that's over," he said sternly.

"I can still choose to leave," she said, hoping the words would bite him so he'd realize what he was saying. His face dropped into one of dark anger.

"If you will not listen to me, you *can* leave," his voice was like the grave, and it stung her.

"Father-"

"I will not have you speaking out against me, I make the decisions, I would rather have you married with him than unmarried with nothing but a dream of romance," her father was red faced in anger.

"Then I'll leave!" she shot back, the words slipped past her lips before she could catch them.

The air between them was still and quiet.

The moment stretched thinly, until a cough in the next room let Anna know her mother was nearby. She had a habit of listening in on conversations, and Anna couldn't hold it against her.

"I'll be gone by tomorrow night," Anna added, the words terrifying and unreal feeling even as she said them.

***

She didn't sleep that night.

Anna spent the night shoving what she could into a couple bags. Her clothing was plain, but plenty. She wasn't sure what she was planning on doing, on where she was planning on going. She just knew that if she spent another night under the same roof as her father she was going to explode.

Samuel wasn't an option.

In the blue light of morning she heard her father leave for his work.

Out her window she watched him pause for a moment, looking towards her window, and then step up onto his buggy and leave.

Just as well, she reminded herself, it would be easier to leave if he wasn't there.

As she started to drag her two bags to the front, her mother stopped her.

"Anna," her mother said, soothing a hand over Anna's right arm. "Are you sure you want to do this?" she asked softly.

"No," Anna admitted. "The only thing I'm sure I want in this world is that I do not want to be with Samuel," she explained.

"You could stay, reason with him, be patient with your father," her mother said gently.

"You know better than I do that's not an option," Anna sighed. "It's easier this way, otherwise I know I'd end up marrying Samuel," she explained.

"Alright," her mother replied. "You should take this though," she added, handing a small envelope to Anna. "It'll get you through long enough until you get a job," she tucked her arms tight around Anna. "You can always come back to me, my Anna, your father is stubborn but he'll miss you," she explained.

"He'll not want me back after this," Anna argued, feeling tears prickle at her eyes.

"You're his daughter, he always will have a spot for you," she countered,

"Thank you, mother," Anna sobbed, rubbing her eyes as the tears free fell.

"Of course my daughter," her mother answered, hugging her again. "I love you very much, I'll do anything for you to be happy," she added.

When her mother set to starting to clean laundry for the day, Anna was forced to start her journey.

The world looked too ordinary, too regular, for what day it was.

She steeled herself, and started her walk out of the village she'd always lived in. Out to where she knew cars would take her to a city, to a place so impossibly different and strange to her.

Anything was better than Samuel, though.

Chapter Two

Within her first week she'd already gone through over half of the three thousand her mother left her.

Anna was an intelligent girl, though. She'd found a room to rent in a Victorian home, something not too unfamiliar from what homes she was used to, for just a couple hundred a month. She paid six months of it in advance, and spent the rest on clothes, food, and a phone, to make herself to fit in.

Her new landlady, Holly, was to thank for most of the ideas and shopping.

She was a forty year old woman, and so kind, Anna was thankful she'd found her listing in the news paper. Not everything was as unfamiliar as she'd imagined.

People treated her differently, but as long as she ignored them they'd have nothing to say.

A couple men had talked to her, shown interest in her, but she had ignored all of them. She was sure she was being rude, she was sure that she'd never make any friends this way, but she also was sure that friendship wasn't what these men were wanting.

She'd never date.

Never go after any men, or marry.

She'd decided this on the ride out from her home.

Anna knew that she'd never find a man, an English man, who her parents would approve of. She couldn't marry someone they didn't approve of, even if she wasn't a part of the church anymore. In her heart she knew it would be the wrong thing to do.

She loved the idea of love, of finding someone who you match with perfectly, but she couldn't feel right being in that kind of love if it meant her family would look down on her for it.

She already had enough shame to bear.

The only thing left to do was to find a job.

Holly had gathered a list of places for Anna to look. Everything ranging from lawyer's offices, to factories that made holiday chocolate all year round.

She'd bought comfortable shoes, though, and she was happy to go to each business and try to impress with what she could. There wasn't much on her resume, but she had to try.

If not she'd have squandered her mother's money for nothing.

The general response to her from most companies was an extreme naked curiosity. They'd look at her like she grew a few extra heads during the conversation, and keep her there to talk to them for a bit. Just when she'd think she was closing the deal on the job, most places would apologize and say they were looking for someone with more experience.

She took that to mean they wanted someone who could operate a computer.

Her courage was waning, she wanted to get hired quickly, to be able to send her mother back a return of what she'd been given. Nothing was turning up, though, after a week and a half of, almost constant, searching.

Fearful for what was leftover of the money, not wanting to let herself have too much access to it, Anna found herself inside a bank.

The building was cold, refreshing against the summer sun, and empty besides her and a teller behind one of the long counters.

He caught her eyes, and a curdling guild set low in her stomach immediately.

He was gorgeous.

This stranger, with a name tag that shimmered out Andre, held her attention with more strength than Samuel had in any of the time she'd known him. His curly brown hair was combed back away from strong cheekbones and glittering green eyes. His shoulders looked broad, strong, and he seemed taller than most men she'd seen in the city.

When he looked up back at her, Anna felt chills run through her, and her face heated.

She didn't need to think about that, though, she was on a mission.

"Good afternoon," he greeted, setting aside the papers he was looking at. His voice was deep, echoing in the empty bank.

"Good afternoon," she mirrored. "I was hoping to open an account," she said, unsure how to phrase this. She regretted not asking Holly for help on this.

"I can help you with that," he smiled, turning to his computer. "Checking or savings?" he asked, typing.

"Checking, please," she responded, letting her eyes fall on his hands for just a moment before she looked away.

"Do you have two kinds of identification?" he asked, his typing stopped.

"Yes," she answered, pulling out the state ID she'd gotten just in the last week, and her birth certificate.

He accepted them and then froze.

"Are you Amish?" he asked, he looked stunned. "Or- were- you Amish?" he corrected himself, something nobody else had done.

"I was," she agreed. Her birth certificate named the only Amish town within a hundred miles.

"I was as well," he said, his eyes shining with nostalgia.

"You were?" she said, surprised for once.

"Yes, I was with a town in Idaho, I've been out of the church for five years," he answered.

"I just left the church almost two weeks ago," Anna said meekly.

"Well, welcome to the madness," he replied, a joke in his voice. She immediately felt comfortable with him.

This had never happened to her before.

"Thank you," she answered, unsure of the proper reply.

"I'll go ahead and set up your account," he started typing her information into the computer. "Will you want to use direct deposit for your job?" he asked, handing back her documents.

"I don't have a job yet," she admitted, embarrassed.

He typed something, and then paused for a moment.

"Have you applied here?" he asked.

"No," she answered, embarrassed at herself for overlooking the opportunity.

"We've been holding walk-in interviews, I can get the manager over to talk with you, if you'd like," he offered. "They're very happy to train, here," he said.

"That would be amazing," Anna said, surprised at her own luck.

As she watched him walk away, she could feel herself getting quickly attached. She knew she'd promised herself she'd stay away from boys.

She'd sworn she wouldn't date.

Still, she felt an attraction, an interest in him, that she'd never felt with anyone else. If she was going to live an English life, she owed herself to at least properly try it.

***

The interview was simple.

An older man, older than her father, asked her a handful of questions about her life an experience. He didn't seem phased that she'd never touched a computer until the last couple of weeks.

She stood up as the interview ended, expecting him to say they were looking for someone with more experience.

"Would you be available to start training tomorrow?" he asked instead, opening the door into for her.

"Yes!"

Chapter Three

Working with Andre was testing her convictions.

He was placed in charge of training her, helping her figure out the computers and the cash counting machines. Andre was patient, kind, and took his time with her even when customers were around.

She learned he'd moved into the state right after he left the church. He didn't own a television, but watched shows on a computer he had a home. She learned he liked to order lunch in, but always forgot to eat breakfast.

She learned he was incredibly generous with his smiles.

Regardless of how simple, how quick, her attachment to him had been within the first couple minutes of meeting him, it had grown into something stronger.

They bonded over talking about similar life experiences, over finding out what differences set them apart. He'd ridden in cars a lot growing up, none owned by his family, while she'd never been in a computer until the last couple weeks.

He was like a piece of her home that she'd left behind.

A warm blanket in the starkness of the new world she was getting used to.

A couple weeks into working together he asked her to dinner, and she couldn't make herself say no.

He picked a place close to her home, and she was both thrilled and terrified.

Holly immediately took the helm.

"I haven't dated in ten years, but you make me feel like I'm the one going out to night," Holly laughed, helping her pick out something to wear. "It's so funny that you're both Amish, isn't it?" she asked, Anna couldn't see the humor, but she nodded anyways.

"I think blue is really the best color for you," Holly said, pulling back Anna's hair so that it didn't cover the simple dress too much.

"Thank you," Anna said.

"But- are you sure you don't want to wear something brighter? Something turquoise and bright would really catch his eye," Holly offered, looking her over.

"No, for him I'd prefer to be myself," Anna smiled.

"Mm, alright," Holly tapped her shoulder, and Anna leaned her head back to let her braid her hair. They'd grown close very quickly, and Anna was glad to have someone in her corner. "He may be Amish, but he's still a boy, if you need anything please call me," Holly said, pausing to look Anna over in the mirror again. "You're gonna knock his socks off," she added, smiling.

***

The restaurant was busy when Anna arrived. She was early, so she requested a table, and then sat there and stared at the crowd.

She couldn't imagine what kinds of lives everyone in that building led. Jobs she'd probably never heard of, homes and cars that would blow her mind, problems she couldn't fathom. She couldn't imagine growing up in a world like this.

Anna listened to small snippets of conversations, catching foreign sounding ideas and words, until Andre arrived.

She was the one blown away.

He looked like he'd stepped out of a magazine. She was suddenly stunned to remember that he'd started out like her.

He'd integrated so well into this world that nobody around them would ever guess that he was Amish.

With her, she was sure people would figure it out.

He was amazing.

"Sorry I'm a little late, my Uber got lost," he apologized, sitting across from her.

"It's fine," she shook her head, smiling. She wasn't quite sure what an Uber was, but she told herself she'd ask him later.

The beginning of the date was jittery, she was nervous, and he seemed to be able to tell. She wanted to make a good impression, but was terrified that trying too hard would make her look like she'd forgotten her parents and church.

By the time they finished eating, though, she'd calmed down.

"Why did you leave the church, if I can ask," he said, stacking their plates he slid them to the end of the table.

"Oh, um," Anna wasn't sure how to explain it. She couldn't say she refused marriage, it would look like she'd never wanted to date anyone ever, but she knew she really wanted to date Andre. "My father and I had a disagreement, and he told me to leave," she explained, feeling shame at the explanation.

"Oh, I'm sorry," he said sincerely.

"It's fine," she lied. "I'm enjoying seeing what life out here is like," she admitted.

"I'm glad you're having a good time," he smiled. "So you'd rather be out here?" he asked.

"I'm not sure about that," she shook her head. "I just couldn't stay there," she tried to explain.

"Ah, I completely understand that," he agreed, take one last sip of his water.

"What about you? Why are you out here?" she asked.

"Mm, same thing, disagreements," he said. Anna wondered, her heart in her stomach, if he'd had a similar experience to her. She tried to picture him being forced into marriage, and the idea made her ache for him.

She was glad that his experiences led to him being in front of her, but was upset that it meant he had to be away from his family and the church.

"I want to go back, though," he admitted.

"Really?" Anna was surprised.

"Yes, of course, maybe not the same town, or the same people, but I miss the church. There's no sense of community or wholeness out here, I miss that so much it hurts," he explained.

"Oh," she said, surprised by him again.

She hadn't considered going back.

She'd only been gone a couple of weeks, and although she missed her family and connections she still felt better out in the world than stuck being married to Samuel. If he wanted to go back then her flirting with him was pointless. She wouldn't return with him and risk her father being disappointed in her.

Anna confirmed with herself that she was better off when she had sworn off dating.

When she finally decided this, looking back up at Andre he seemed concerned.

"What's wrong?" he asked, setting down his drink.

"Oh, nothing, I was just thinking about home," she lied.

"I get that," he nodded, continuing to eat.

She's have to stop seeing him.

Have to stop talking to him outside of professionally.

If he fell for her she'd end up hurting him and disappointing her family.

Anna continued to eat as she berated herself. If she was more thoughtful, more intelligent, she would have saved everyone a lot of heartache.

She'd tasted human interaction and became a glutton for it.

Chapter Four

It was harder to ignore Andre than she thought.

First of all, they worked together on every shift- which meant that he'd be within ten feet of her for most of an eight hour shift. Within the first half hour of their first shift together the following Monday he seemed to notice something had changed.

At first he spared her the embarrassment of asking her why.

They worked silently together, he helped her if she needed it, but kept his tone formal and plain. She did the same even though it hurt.

She wasn't sure why it hurt so much.

Anna hadn't known him for even a month, but looking at him and knowing she couldn't talk to him comfortably- knowing she couldn't hold his eye contact- anymore hurt her.

The first week of working together like this was like torture for her. He was a cold drink that her parched throat could never have. Their boss told them that their productivity was up and they had been doing a great job, and it was almost embarrassing. Had she been so distracted that she didn't work her best when she was talking to him?

Had she let him steal away her mind that much?

Anna was sure that the worst had passed. She was sure that he'd let go of his feelings for her, and she of hers, and that they could move on as regular coworkers. It wasn't something she was sure she wanted, and it hurt, but she told herself that it was for the best.

On the next Monday when she went in, someone was in Andre's spot besides him.

It was Kat, from the weekend, and some evening, shifts.

"Where's Andre?" Anna asked, trying to keep herself from seeming invested in the answer.

"He's out sick," Kat said, filling her drawer for the morning rush. "He called in last night," she added.

Anna's heart ached.

"What's wrong with him?" she asked.

"A flu probably," Kat guessed, shrugging. "Can you get me a couple more pens for my station before you get back here?" she asked.

"Yes, of course," Anna said, walking to the storage area.

He was sick.

He was sick and she didn't know? Her own stomach was turning and aching in fear. If she was over him why did it scare her so much just to hear he had the flu?

Why would she care so deeply?

Anna grabbed the pens and headed out.

She'd visit him after her shift.

***

Anna shouldn't have been able to get his home address.

She could have called him ahead and asked for it, but instead she asked Kat for help. If she called him her resolve would break. Anna just wanted to bring him some food and make sure he was okay. She wasn't going to stay long, she wasn't going to let herself say more than twenty words.

That's all.

She stood in front of his apartment complex, staring down the front of it like she was looking for answers.

Why did she care so much?

Why was a bag of hot soup and bread in her hand, why was she standing in front of a random man's home instead at her own home eating her own dinner? Why did it matter if he was okay?

At first she tried to convince herself that it was because he was Amish too, and that she was seeking that familial connection the entire Amish community shares. She knew that wasn't true. She knew better than to lie to herself.

Anna buzzed his room's number from the dial pad, and waited patiently.

"Hello?" he sounded sleepy and her heart warmed.

"I heard you were sick, I've brought food," eight words, she counted as she spoke them.

"I'll be right down," his voice chirped out quickly, like he was surprised. Anna was relieved he hadn't asked her to come up to him instead, she didn't want to appear to be straying any further from her convictions than she had.

"Hey," he said, opening the door after a minute. He looked ruffled, his hair askew and his shirt wrinkled. Her heart warmed at the sight of him, even when he was sick he was still handsome.

"Hi," nine words. She begged for her voice not to betray her.

"Come in, just to the lobby," he said gently, opening the door further. Anna knew she shouldn't but she did anyways.

"How are you feeling?" thirteen words. She could only allow herself seven more. If she went any further she didn't trust herself.

"A lot better," he said, fixing his hair with his hands. "I slept it off most of the day, drank a lot of tea and had a hot bath," he explained. "I should be back at work tomorrow," he added.

"That's good to hear," three words left.

"Yeah," he answered. Then paused for a moment and looked her seriously in the eyes. Anna felt like he was staring right into her mind. "How are you? You've been- different- this last week," he said. Anna considered her words carefully.

"I've been fine," she answered.

Twenty.

She needed to keep her mouth shut.

"Okay," he said gently. A silence hung between them, she knew he expected her to say more, she willed her mouth shut.

Anna handed him the bag of food, and then stepped back towards the door.

"Bye, then," he said, unsure.

Anna nodded, her hand on the handle to open it.

"Anna-" he said gently. She froze, not sure what to do. "Have I done something wrong? Have I hurt you in some way? If so, I'm sorry, I'll ask to be transferred to another location," he offered. "I've really enjoyed getting to know you, I'm sorry f I've made you unhappy," he continued.

Anna's hand tightened on the handle of the door as she felt her resolve start to unravel. He started to step away, and any less will power she had completely dissolved into the air.

"I can't go back and live there," she said softly, feeling tears prickle at her eyes. "I was foolish and got into a fight with my father, I refused to marry someone they wanted me to, and I ran off like a child," she explained, actually crying now. "You want to go back, and I can't give you that, I can't," she explained, shaking. "If I go back there my father won't care, he'll make me marry this stranger," she explained.

"Have you talked to him since then?" Andre asked, walking back to her. "It sounds like you both jumped into it quickly, have you talked about it?"

"I've only sent letters to my mother," Anna shook her head.

"I'm not even sure your town would accept me," Andre said gently.

"What?"

"Come sit down," he motioned to a couple chairs in the lobby. Anna nodded and wiped the tears from her eyes. She never thought she'd like him this much.

Never even considered it.

"I was forced to leave because my village was convinced that I stole something from a brother of mine, even though I was out of town when it happened," he explained. "He told them I stole and sold one of their horses to the English, and they believed him. I was made to leave within a week," he explained.

"You wouldn't do that," she gasped, disgusted someone would spread a story like that.

"No, I wouldn't," he agreed. "My brother was always greed, though, and my father just recently passed. Their house was to be mine, and now it's his," he said.

"That's awful," Anna shook her head, upset.

"It's how it is," Andre shrugged. "I won't make you go anywhere you don't want to, I won't make you do anything you don't want to, but please don't shut me out like that anymore," he said gently.

"Okay," Anna nodded, feeling drained and embarrassed.

He was too kind, too understanding.

"I want to speak to my father," she admitted.

"Want me to be there for it?" he offered.

"Maybe," she sighed, wiping the last of the moisture off her face. "You should eat," she added.

"Alright," he stood slowly, walking her to the door. "Thank you for talking to me."

"Of course," she said, feeling foolish for treating him how she did.

Andre leaned down and kissed her forehead gently, before opening the door for her. Anna could feel her heart rushing the whole walk home.

What did she want?

Chapter Five

She was in front of her home again.

Regardless of where she went, who she was in the world, this place would always be her home.

She'd waited the entire week, had pressured herself into patience as she tried to figure out what to say. She wasn't asking to marry Andre, he hadn't asked her, but she wanted to court him.

She wanted her parents to be a part of her life.

She couldn't silence how she felt about them, she couldn't hide what her mind was doing.

She just wanted them to know how she felt.

Anna plucked up her courage and knocked on the door for the first time in her life. Before this she'd always been able to just go in. Before now this was always where she lived.

It was evening, the sun starting to drip down onto the horizon as the air cooled. Long blue shadows painted the fields and homes, and in the glow she felt nostalgic. There were footsteps inside, and she waited patiently, her heart hammering in her ears.

"Anna?" her mother gasped as she opened the door. Anna was swept into her arms, pulled tight and close, and Anna could feel the shudder of her mother starting to cry. "I thought all I'd ever see of you anymore was letters," her mother sobbed out, clutching her against herself.

"No, no, I'm here," Anna answered, hugging her back. She could feel tears pricking against her own eyes. "I need to speak to father," Anna said gently.

"He has hardly spoken since you left," her mother admitted wearily.

"Then I just need him to listen," Anna replied. She felt like she'd aged years since she had been there last, even though it had been less than two months.

"Alright," her mother nodded, patting her arm and pulling Anna into the home.

The house smelled of dinner and dishes, her mother had been cleaning when Anna arrived, and it took all of her willpower not to distract herself into helping clean.

"Anna is here," her mother said as they entered the sitting room. Her father was there, the bible in his lap. When he looked up at her, his eyes seemed so sad. Her heart broke for him.

"Father," Anna said gently, moving to sit next to him on the couch. He watched her quietly, only breaking his silence to itch his beard. She could remember growing up and pulling on his beard as a young girl. He looked so old now. "I'd like to talk to you for a short while," she explained. He nodded, and glanced up at her mother, who then went back to the kitchen to continue cleaning.

"You're not wearing English clothing," he noted.

"I'm not English," she reminded him. It was good to hear his voice. "I want to apologize for going wild as I did, and not listening to you," she explained. "I don't regret not marrying Samuel, but I do regret arguing with you and disrespecting you." He was quiet as she spoke, listening to each word she said with immense consideration.

"I have met an Amish man while I've been out there, and I wish to court him," she explained simply. "I'm not here to beg you to accept him, or to tell you that I wish to marry him, I just don't want to keep any part of my life from you," she said. Her father nodded.

"Who is this man?" he asked, his voice was patient, not accusing.

"He's a coworker of mine at a bank, he's kinda and intelligent," she answered.

"He's Amish?"

"Yes, and he wants to join the church again and it will have him," she said. "I want to come home father, he wants to come with me, I miss my family and world," she explained.

Her father was quiet for a while, mulling over everything he just heard. Anna was patient and watched him carefully. Her mother walked by the outside of the room more often than was necessary, she knew she was listening for an answer as well.

Her father took her hand gently and stared down at it.

"Your mother has missed you," he said softly. She knew that he meant he did as well, she didn't question it. "When I chased you away like I did I was brash, I wasn't thinking about what was best for everyone," he explained. "I wanted you to have marriage, to have happiness, like your mother and I have found. I didn't consider that Samuel would ever make you unhappy," he continued. "I'll meet this man," he explained.

Anna reached forward and grasped her father into her arms. She hadn't hugged him in years, hadn't thought to, but she needed to hold her father. His arms wrapped around her as well, and she felt like a child again.

"I just want you to be happy," he said, his voice went weak for a moment, and she willed herself to ignore it. If her father cried, she's save him the embarrassment of knowing she'd seen it.

"I'm sorry I didn't treat you with the respect you've earned," she responded, holding him tight.

They sat there for a moment, reunited and feeling every inch of how apart they were.

"When can I meet him?" her father asked, leaning back away from her. There was a shine to her eyes that she felt her heart warm to.

"He's outside. He dressed in clothes he still had from his last town, he's waiting just outside of the fence," she admitted, bowing her head. "He requested to meet you both," she added. Her mother now stopped in the hall, no longer pretending she was carrying laundry back and forth for the tenth time. Setting down the basket, she approached the two of them and sat her hands on her husbands shoulder.

"We'll see him," her father said, nodding.

Anna nodded, and rushed out to get him.

"They want to see you," she said gently, pulling him out of his thoughts. Anxious nerves and excitement both crossed Andre's face, and she ached to wipe the lines of stress away.

"My father has forgiven me, we're okay now," she added, trying to soothe him.

"Alright," he said, taking her hand. "I love you," he added, the crickets around them were humming to life as the sun began to really set.

"I love you too," she breathed out, amazed that the words were hers, that she really meant them.

She couldn't fear anything, nothing was scary anymore.

She was in love, and her parents accepted it.

As she led him back to the house, her hand brushing against his, glad to finally be back home.

One Amish Summer

SAMANTHA COLLIER

One Amish Summer

The wide plains of Pennsylvania were like undulating waves, tossing over Delilah. She had never seen the sea, but she imagined that it must be like this: never ending, eternal. She felt alone, in the vast landscape.

They had been travelling for a few hours, and she was starting to despair. When would they arrive in at their destination? She had never travelled so far, and for so long. Any trips that her family had made over the years she had been exempt from, because of her health. Her mother had always said that she simply wasn't up to long trips. And so, Delilah had always been left behind, in the care of relatives.

Until now. Now, she was going to stay with her aunt, over the summer period. And all by herself. Her father was taking her there, but he would return home almost immediately.

The buggy jolted over the unfamiliar terrain. Her father frowned, righting the carriage. He wasn't used to this area of the country, either. And she knew that he was doing it under sufferance, at her mother's insistence. He had work to do; he didn't want to take time out of his schedule for this trip. As always, Delilah felt herself a burden.

She didn't even know why her mother had insisted so vehemently. She would have been happier staying at home; she had never sought this out. Yes, it would be nice to catch up with her Aunt Mildred and her cousin Katura, but she had never been with them for long periods of time. She didn't know what to expect.

Delilah had been thrust out of the comfortable bubble that she had lived in all of her life, and she was apprehensive.

At last. Her father turned down a dirt track, and Delilah could see the farmhouse in the distance. As they approached closer, she saw two figures in long blue dresses and crisp white aprons on the front veranda, waiting for them.

"Whoa." Her father drew in the reins, causing the horses to stop sharply. And then, the two figures were running down the steps to greet them.

"You made it!" Aunt Mildred was upon them. Delilah noticed her familiar lopsided smile, and also that her aunt looked older. Her hair had gone almost completely grey. Well, it had been five years since they had last seen each other.

By her side was Delilah's cousin, Katura. Delilah drew in her breath, sharply, when she observed her cousin. In the five years since she had seen her, Katura had grown from a lanky teenager into a well-rounded, confident looking woman. Her smile was bright, and everything about her – her stance, her mannerisms – spoke volumes. Katura knew her place in the world, and her value.

Delilah immediately felt insecure, even more so than usual. How must she appear to them? Had she changed, as well? But she knew, in her heart, that she hadn't blossomed in the same way that her cousin had. She was still the frail, sickly looking girl she had always been.

"Come in, come in," her aunt was saying now. "Welcome!"

Greetings exchanged, they all made their way into the farmhouse. Delilah looked around, entranced. She had never been here before. For the first time, she allowed a tiny stab of excitement enter her heart at the prospect of staying the summer here.

"How was your trip?" Aunt Mildred was bustling around, serving them coffee and cakes.

"Tolerable," her father answered. "We took the back roads where we could, but we couldn't avoid some major ones. The traffic was fierce in some spots." He smiled, a bit wearily. Again, Delilah felt guilty. It was a familiar feeling; she was always demanding attention from her parents, even though she never sought it.

"Well, you are here safely," her aunt answered. "That is all that matters." She turned to her niece, her eyes quietly assessing her. "It is so lovely to see you again, Delilah. We are delighted to have you for the summer."

"Thank you, Auntie," Delilah answered, dismayed as always by how soft her voice was. Why couldn't she be louder, more assertive? "I am pleased to be here. I am looking forward to the visit."

Aunt Mildred smiled. "You will have a great time, I am sure," she said. "Katura will take you under her wing, show you about the district. You have much planned, don't you, Katura?"

Her cousin smiled, but it didn't reach her eyes. "Of course, Mamm," she said, in a bored voice. She didn't once glance at Delilah. "Depending on how well Delilah feels, of course."

This was how it had always been. Everyone always had to make allowances for her health. No wonder Katura already looked burdened with it. She probably had her own plans for the summer, and now she had to mind her sickly cousin.

"How is your health, Delilah?" Aunt Mildred asked. "Have you improved at all?"

"Much, thank you, Aunt," Delilah answered, casting anxious eyes towards her cousin. "I can't do any vigorous physical activities, but I can go for short walks, longer than before." She turned to Katura. "I will try to keep up with you, cousin."

Katura snorted. "So no swimming or camping, then?" she said. Her eyes looked disdainful. "My friends and I were planning a trip next week, but I suppose I must decline." She sighed, a tad dramatically.

There was an awkward silence at the table. Delilah felt her heart plummet in her chest. This was not a good start to the visit. Her cousin already resented her for being there.

"I am sure there will be lots that Delilah can do," Aunt Mildred nodded her head, decisively. "We will just have to think it through." Almost as an afterthought she turned to her niece. "You are most welcome here, Delilah." Then her eyes turned to her own daughter. Waves of disapproval emanated from her. "Katura is also very glad to have you here."

"Very glad," echoed Katura. Delilah wasn't fooled; her cousin wouldn't even look at her.

Delilah felt the familiar dread. She had made a mistake. She should never have let her mother talk her into this trip. She had spoilt everyone's summer.

But it was all too late, now.

***

Her father had left, declining the offer for lunch. "I must get back," he had said. He turned to Delilah, taking her hands in his. "I hope you have a wonderful time, daughter." Then he had put his black hat on his head and departed.

She was shown to the room that she would stay in, up the stairs, opposite Katura's. It was a good sized room, with a wrought iron single bed covered by a colourful quilt. The window showed a view out to the valley, and beyond.

As she unpacked, she lamented her weakly constitution. It had always got in the way.

She remembered when it had happened. Before that, she had been the same as every other child, able to climb and run outside. She had been boisterous, and happy.

It had been a bitterly cold winter, the year that she had turned eight. So cold; Delilah could still remember shivering in her bed, despite layers of quilts. A virus had spread through the district, felling almost everyone in its path. It particularly struck the weak; old people with little immunity were keeling over from it.

When it had entered their house, she had been struck the worst. A very bad influenza, that racked her body. Her mother had tended her almost around the clock. And then, it had gotten worse. Pneumonia.

She could still remember how panicked she had felt, that she was unable to draw breath. She had felt that was drowning in the fluids in her lungs. And the fever! Half the time she had been delirious, not knowing where she was. She remembered her mother and father standing at the doorway to her room, their brows knotted with worry.

She had recovered, slowly. But the pneumonia had left its mark. It had scarred her lungs, and she simply was never the same again. She could no longer climb and run, as she once had. Most of the time, she stayed in the living room, a rug over her knees. She became known as delicate; the friends that she had once had no longer came to play. Her own brothers and sisters would run off outside, and they never asked her to join them, anymore. Even if they had, her mother wouldn't have allowed it.

Delilah frowned, remembering. Had her mother been over protective? Could she have done more, or at least, been encouraged to? She knew that her parents worried about her, so much. She thought now that they had probably wrapped her in cotton wool. Which was why she had never been on any long trips, before.

"Are you unpacked?"

Delilah glanced up from what she was doing. It was Katura.

"*Jah*, all done," she answered, looking at her cousin. "I am sorry, Katura. I don't want to be a burden."

Katura's gaze softened slightly. "Don't be silly," she sniffed. "Can you sing? After service tomorrow, the Evening Sing is happening. I'd like you to come. There's a young man I've got my eye on."

"Really?" Delilah smiled. "What is his name?"

"Isaiah King," Katura breathed. "He is wonderful! I think that he is going to ask me to court, soon."

Katura sat down on the bed, and regaled Delilah with everything about this Isaiah: his manners, his history, and his appearance. Judging by her cousin's shining eyes, Delilah could tell that Katura was serious about him.

She listened and nodded, but all the while felt sadness. It was ridiculous. She should be happy for her cousin. But self-pity overwhelmed Delilah.

She would never be courted, or asked to marry. She would never have a family or a home of her own, despite what her mother thought. Delilah knew that one reason her mother had insisted on this trip was in the vain hope that Delilah might meet somebody. No young man in her own district ever paid her a shred of attention, and why should they? She was known as sickly. She couldn't do the things that everyone else could. What man would want a semi invalid for a wife? They wanted strong, vibrant girls who could work alongside them.

If she were honest, Delilah knew that her mother had half created the situation, by being so over protective. Maybe Delilah could have done more, or been pushed to at least try.

No, love wasn't for her. Love was for girls like Katura, who shone with energy and life. Delilah was destined to be a spinster, forever sitting in her parents' home, wasting away year after year.

She shouldn't resent her cousin. It was unkind; God wouldn't like it. He didn't look kindly on girls who felt sorry for themselves. Acceptance, Delilah thought. I must accept my lot in life, and not dream of anything more.

With her resolve in place, Delilah turned to her cousin, and let herself truly feel excited for her.

"I can't wait to meet Isaiah," she told her.

***

Delilah glanced around the unfamiliar barn, and the unfamiliar faces singing to heaven. Her heart was pounding, painfully. She wasn't used to being in crowds, and certainly not amongst unfamiliar people. The only person she knew at this Evening Sing was Katura, and of course her cousin knew everybody.

Her cousin nudged her, staring over at a young man further down. Judging by her cousin's shining eyes, the young man was him. Isaiah King. The one that Katura was sure was about to ask her to start courting.

Delilah studied him. He was indeed handsome, and his eyes shone with kindness. She felt a stirring, an unfamiliar feeling entering her soul. She frowned – what was she thinking? Her cousin was sweet on this man. Delilah shook her head, trying to dislodge the feeling.

And yet it stayed with her, all through the hymns. A sweet, yearning feeling that she had simply never felt before.

The hymns over, everyone got up. Katura took Delilah's arm, leading her over to Isaiah.

"Isaiah," her cousin breathed. He turned around, looking at them both.

His eyes widened as he looked at Delilah. She felt herself blushing; it seemed to take over her, feeling much like a fever.

"This is my cousin, Delilah," Katura said. "She is staying with us for the summer."

The young man held out his hand. "Greetings, Delilah. Welcome to our district."

She took his hand, shaking it. Did he hang onto it just a tad too long? He was certainly staring at her. Delilah glanced nervously at Katura. Her cousin was frowning.

Delilah broke the contact abruptly. "Thank you," she said, awkwardly.

Another young man had come over to them, looking at them expectantly. Delilah turned to look at him. His eyes were cold, and he wasn't smiling.

"Isaiah, we must away," the other young man said. "You know how early a start we have tomorrow."

Isaiah sighed. "Of course," he said. "But you must meet the young lady who is visiting us for the summer. Delilah, this is my brother, Jeremiah."

Jeremiah barely glanced at her. He was frowning. "*Jah*, nice to meet you," he said. He turned back to Isaiah. He looked like he couldn't wait a minute longer.

"Well, I'm sure we will see each other again," Isaiah said to her. He looked at her one last time, then seemed to remember that Katura was standing there, looking at him. "Katura, are you coming swimming with us, over at the lake next week?"

"I would," Katura answered. "But Delilah can't swim, and my mother insists that I don't do anything without her." Was there a little eye roll as she spoke? Delilah's face burned again.

"But Delilah must come," Isaiah smiled. "Of course you must."

"Oh, I have never learnt to swim..." Her voice trailed off. How pathetic must she sound?

"You can still enjoy the day, can't you?" He smiled. "Even if you can't swim, you can sit and be in nature, surely?"

"Well..." Delilah looked at Katura, a bit desperately. How should she respond?

"It's settled, then." Isaiah put his hat on his head. "I will pick both of you up this Thursday."

"Isaiah." Jeremiah was impatiently looking toward the door.

"Coming." With a last glance back at the girls, Isaiah left with his brother.

Katura sighed, deeply. "See, what a wonderful man he is?" she said to her cousin. "Including you, just because of me! You must come, Delilah. As Isaiah said, you can watch."

Delilah nodded, slowly. She didn't seem to have much choice. And she had wanted to join in, hadn't she? She had dreamed of being able to participate, and be included.

And then, there was the thought of seeing Isaiah again. Her heart started to beat slowly at the thought.

What was wrong with her? Her cousin liked him. She would pray, that God would stop this feeling. It felt wrong. Even though she knew it hardly mattered – it wasn't as if Isaiah would ever consider her in that way, even if he had no interest at all in Katura.

****

"Isaiah! Stop splashing!"

Delilah watched from the bank, as the group of young people splashed in the water. Oh, how she longed to be able to join in! The water looked so inviting, especially on this hot day. She was sweating.

Katura was laughing, enjoying herself. Delilah watched her look at Isaiah from beneath her eyelashes, making every excuse to be near him. Delilah didn't think that Isaiah looked at Katura in any special way; he was equally friendly with everybody. Had her cousin misread his regard for her?

She watched his brother, Jeremiah, off by himself. He didn't seem to want to join in with the others. He gazed over the lake, seemingly deep in thought. He didn't look happy. Delilah felt a dark wave go over her. Why didn't she like him? There was just a feeling she got. As much as she had felt a glow when she had first met Isaiah, she felt a darkness around Jeremiah.

She had always been intuitive about people. It was like she could read them, straight away. Maybe it was her spells of illness; it had heightened her senses, in some way. She had always been an observer of life, rather than a participant.

The swimmers waded out now, laughing. But Jeremiah stayed by himself in the water, a dark cloud hanging over his head.

Isaiah looked at Delilah. "Are you enjoying yourself?" he asked her, smiling. "It is such a beautiful day." His eyes locked into hers. Delilah didn't think that she had ever seen such blue eyes before. They seemed to sear into her soul, touching her inside.

"Delilah," he said, seeming at a loss of words. He looked over his shoulder at Katura, who had wondered along the bank with some other people. "I was wondering whether you might like to accompany me to a restaurant in town, next week?" He looked down, blushing.

Delilah's breath caught in her throat. "With Katura, you mean?"

"*Nein*," he shook his head, gazing at her again. "I mean, just you and I."

Was he asking her to court? Delilah couldn't believe it; had she imagined the words? She stared at him, dumbfounded.

"But...but..." she stammered. "Don't you like Katura? She likes you."

Isaiah looked back at Katura. "I know she does," he sighed. "But I like her just as a friend." He gazed at her, intently. "The minute I saw you, Delilah, I knew. That we had a connection. Can you deny it?"

She shook her head, slowly. She had felt it, too, instantly, but she had dismissed it. She wasn't used to it, and besides, Katura liked him.

"I just don't know," she whispered. She could see Katura looking over at them, frowning. Oh dear Lord, what was she doing?

"Think about it," Isaiah said. "There isn't anything between Katura and I, despite what she may wish. There would be no betrayal of her, if that is what makes you hesitate."

"I will think about it," Delilah whispered.

Isaiah smiled. "Jeremiah, Samuel and I are going to do a spot of fishing, now," he said. "Maybe you can tell me your decision when we all meet up, again."

Delilah watched Jeremiah leave the water, staring over at his brother. The other young man, Samuel, had already picked up their fishing rods. "Are you ready, Isaiah?" he called.

"Coming," he called back. He smiled at Delilah, then joined the others. They walked off, into the woods.

"What was Isaiah talking to you about?"

Delilah started. Katura was looming over her. And she didn't look happy.

***

Delilah wondered later, after the events of the day had unfolded, how everything changed in a heartbeat.

Katura had pressed her for details about Isaiah, but Delilah had said that he merely was chatting with her. She knew that she should have told her cousin that Isaiah had asked her out, but she couldn't bring herself to.

They had both sat there, in stony silence, when they heard it.

The scream. A bloodcurdling scream, which seemed to echo around the woods.

Delilah and Katura jumped to their feet, looking at each other fearfully. "What was that?" Katura said. "Is it the men?"

Katura ran off, and Delilah jumped to her feet, following. She couldn't run as fast as the other girl; even now, her breath came in painful rasps. The woods seemed impenetrable. What had happened?

Eventually, she got to where Katura was, standing still. And she saw everything.

Isaiah and Jeremiah, standing there. But Samuel was on the ground, seemingly out cold. The two brothers looked down at him. They both looked like they were in shock.

Delilah didn't think. She simply rushed over to the prone man, crouching over him. His eyes weren't open. And there was a deep gash on his forehead, oozing blood.

"What happened?" Delilah ripped her apron, pressing the material against the head wound, trying desperately to stem the bleeding.

The brothers stood there, looking down. Neither of them spoke.

"Katura," she called. "Can you help?"

Her cousin seemed to come to her senses, rushing over to them. "Dear Lord, is he alive?"

Delilah pressed her face against his chest. "Just barely."

She turned to the two men. "You have to pick him up!" she shouted. "Why are you both standing there? We have to get him to hospital, as quickly as possible."

The two men came over, the spell broken. "*Jah*, of course," said Jeremiah. He picked up Samuel's legs. Isaiah slowly walked around to his head.

"Oh, God," he suddenly cried. His face was ashen. "This is my fault. I did this."

Delilah's heart went cold.

***

It was all like a dream, afterwards. The trip to the hospital. Desperately trying to stem Samuel's bleeding. The questions, none of which she could answer.

And then, as they all sat in the hospital ward, waiting for news about Samuel's condition, the police had arrived.

They had questioned them all, separately.

Delilah had left the room, to get herself a drink of water. She was shaking from delayed shock. The nurses had told her that she had done the right thing, trying to stop the bleeding. She had probably saved Samuel's life, but he wasn't good. He was in a coma, and she could tell by the rushing around, the whispers and frowns, that it might still happen. He might die.

Then the police had taken Isaiah away. Delilah still couldn't believe it. How could he be responsible for this? She didn't know him well, but her instincts had never been wrong about people before. He was a good man, she knew it.

And then, it hit her: she was falling in love with him. She had never thought that it could happen so quickly. She had heard about love at first sight, but always dismissed it as fiction. But it was true: it had happened to her.

And now, she watched helplessly as her new love was dragged away, seemingly about to be charged for this evil act.

She turned to look at Jeremiah. How was he feeling – it was his brother, after all, that had just been taken away by the police.

But Jeremiah sat there, a stony look on his face. A nerve twitched in his brow, but he said nothing. Nothing.

Katura was pale. "Delilah, we should leave," she whispered. "My mother will be worried, we are so late. There is nothing more that we can do here."

Delilah nodded. But she watched Jeremiah as they left, sitting there like a statue. She could almost see the dark cloud over his head.

There was more to this. She just knew it.

***

That night, she and Katura stayed up late, drinking cocoa and trying to make sense of the strange and troubling events of the day.

"I simply can't believe it," Katura whispered, shaking her head. "It is so out of character. I went to school with Isaiah, and I have never once seen any anger or tendency to violence in him. Not once!"

Delilah sipped her cocoa, frowning. "Tell me about Jeremiah. What is he like?"

Katura shuddered. "I have never liked him," she said. "Furtive. Always watching, but not in a good way."

"Have you ever seen him act in a violent manner?"

"No, I don't think so." Katura frowned, thinking. "He is not hot headed. At school, he was always behind the scenes if there were any altercations. I always got the sense that he might be egging things on, but he would never act himself."

Delilah frowned, thinking it through. It was a mystery.

The fact that Isaiah had asked her out, just prior to the incident occurring. He had seemed carefree, happy. What had gone on between the three men, to change everything so drastically? They had set out to fish. It had been a beautiful day.

A vision of Jeremiah in the water came to her. Frowning. Separate.

"And what about Samuel, Katura?" she asked her cousin. "Is he close to both?"

"Samuel is Isaiah's best friend," answered Katura. "They have been inseparable since they were little." She pressed a hand to her forehead. "I cannot think about it anymore. I must go to bed. Will you retire also?"

Delilah smiled faintly at her cousin. "In a moment. I will finish my drink. Good night, dear cousin."

She reached out and took Katura's hand. Her cousin looked surprised, but squeezed it. Then she drifted up the stairs to bed.

Delilah felt so tired she could almost have put her head on the table and slept there. She should go to bed, but her mind was whirring so much she knew that sleep would elude her.

The sudden, world shifting attraction between Isaiah and herself. Then the incident, that Isaiah had taken responsibility for. She still didn't know what had happened; both men refused to speak. Had Isaiah pushed Samuel because of a sudden disagreement, and he had hit his head? Or had the act been more deliberate? But Samuel was his best friend. And Isaiah didn't have that darkness in him; she was sure of it.

And then there was the fact that Jeremiah had said nothing. Not even when the police had taken his brother away.

Was Isaiah covering up for Jeremiah? But, why would he?

Delilah looked at the clock. It was about to chime midnight. There would be no answers tonight. She would think about it tomorrow, with a clear head.

She drifted up the stairs to bed, worry eating at her soul.

***

She tossed and turned all night. When she was asleep, strange, vivid dreams took hold of her.

They were back at the lake. Jeremiah was in the water, way into the distance. She was watching him, her breath getting shallower. Suddenly, she was in the water herself, desperately trying to swim.

"Help me," she cried out. Jeremiah watched her, his face impassive. She knew he had heard her, but he didn't move.

Then, Isaiah was there. "Don't worry," he whispered. "I will save you." Samuel was by his side, nodding. "Trust him, Delilah," he said. "He won't let you down."

She woke up, suddenly. She was indeed gasping for breath. She sat up, and reached over for the glass of water on the bedside table. Her hand was shaking.

Isaiah wasn't guilty. She knew it, now. He could never do such a thing.

But Jeremiah could. She was equally sure of that.

***

Delilah watched Samuel in the hospital bed, hooked up to machines. His eyes were closed; he looked like he was sleeping peacefully. As if his eyelids might flutter suddenly, and he would stretch and awaken.

But it wasn't as simple as that. For Samuel was in a coma, and he mightn't ever awake from it.

And if he didn't, Isaiah would be charged with murder.

Delilah came into the room, resting on her knees beside the bed. She prayed to God, fervently. She prayed that Samuel wouldn't lose his life. He was so young, and had his whole life before him. Delilah didn't know him at all, but she had liked him. She also prayed for Isaiah. She still simply could not believe that he had done this. She prayed that the truth of what had happened would be revealed.

She picked up Samuel's hand. His family had left the room, just five minutes prior. She still felt the awful grief and horror that had been left in their wake. His mother had looked devastated, as if her world had collapsed. And his father had been tight lipped with grief.

"Samuel." She whispered, stroking his hand. "I know I don't know you well. Please wake up. Your family need you. Wake up, Samuel, and tell people what really happened to you. We need to know."

She watched his face, but there wasn't a flicker. The only sound in the room was the beeping of the machines.

Delilah sighed, feeling as low as she had ever felt. She loved Isaiah. Why was he claiming that he had done this? She knew in her heart it simply wasn't true.

She must speak with him.

***

Isaiah looked like he had aged a thousand years. Grief etched his features.

Delilah sat opposite him, across the sparse table at the police station.

"How are you?" she whispered.

He sighed, blinking back tears. "Don't ask me," he responded. "I don't deserve it. I deserve nothing."

Delilah closed her eyes for a moment. "Isaiah, I don't believe you. I know that you couldn't have done this to Samuel."

Isaiah just looked at her, sadly. "I am so sorry, Delilah," he sighed. "For everything. For what could have been, between us. I know it is sudden; I know that we hardly know each other. But I was falling in love with you."

Tears slid down Delilah's face. "I am in love with you, Isaiah. I tried to fight it, because of Katura, but it is what it is. Like what is between us existed before we even knew about it." She wiped the tears away. "And that is how I know that you are innocent. I am very intuitive about people; I knew straight away that you were a good soul. But what about Jeremiah?"

Isaiah looked up at her, sharply. But he didn't say a word.

"What about us?" she pressed. "If you take responsibility for this, we will never have a chance. And your life will be over."

"Don't you think I know that?" He looked haggard. "But family is family. And Jeremiah is my little brother."

Delilah looked at him, sharply. There it was. She knew for sure, now.

Jeremiah had done this. And Isaiah had taken the blame, because he was his baby brother, and he wanted to protect him.

Isaiah was willing to give up his own life, to protect his brother. That was the type of man he was. Delilah wanted to shake him, say that Jeremiah didn't deserve this loyalty; that if he hurt Samuel, he needed to take responsibility for it. That Isaiah wasn't helping him. He was just ruining his own life.

But Isaiah had closed down, and wouldn't speak further. "I am so sorry, Delilah," he whispered. "Please, don't come again. Find a man who deserves you. I pray to God that your life will be happy."

He stood up, and left the room. Delilah watched him leave, her heart breaking.

***

Katura sat with her that night, in the living room.

"I know," she said, turning her head to Delilah. "About you and Isaiah. That you have fallen in love with each other."

Delilah gasped. "How did you know?" she asked. Tears streamed down her face, for the second time that day. "I am so sorry, Katura. I never wanted to hurt you."

"It's okay," whispered Katura. "I think I knew, deep down, that Isaiah wasn't interested in me. And he never gave me any indication that there might be a possibility of the two of us courting. It was all just wishful thinking on my part." She breathed out, deeply. "It's alright, Delilah. You both have my blessing."

Delilah leaned over and hugged her cousin. "It doesn't matter, anyway," she whispered. "Isaiah is determined to take the blame for the incident, and he told me that I should move on. That I should find someone else." She sighed, deeply. "But I never will."

"You don't think Isaiah did it?" said Katura. "You think it was Jeremiah?"

"I do," said Delilah. "But he won't admit it. Why is he doing this?"

Katura smiled, grimly. "There is only the two of them," she said. "Their parents died years ago, and they have no one else in the family. They live together, on their property. Isaiah has always looked out for Jeremiah, protected him."

It made sense, then. Isaiah's overarching loyalty to Jeremiah. A loyalty so strong, he was even prepared to take the blame for something that would ruin his life. And Samuel was his best friend, as well.

"We should pray," whispered Delilah. "It is the only thing that we can do."

Both young women closed their eyes. Delilah prayed harder than she had ever in her life.

***

God answered their prayers.

Aunt Mildred told them the good news as soon as they came down for breakfast. "Girls, Samuel Stoltzfus has woken up!" she said, her eyes shining. "The Lord has heard us."

Delilah and Katura embraced, hugging each other tightly. Tears of joy fell down their faces.

"And you know what else?"

They both looked at her, expectantly.

"Samuel has told the police that Jeremiah pushed him," Aunt Mildred continued. "He said they argued, and Jeremiah just lashed out. Samuel must have hit his head on a rock when he fell." Aunt Mildred lifted her eyes to heaven. "Isaiah has been released from custody."

Delilah gasped. All her prayers had been answered. Isaiah was free! And he hadn't done anything to Samuel. She had known, all along!

She started weeping. Aunt Mildred came over to her, looking at her tenderly.

"I think you should go and see him," she whispered. "I will drive you over there myself."

***

He was standing on the front veranda when they pulled up. Delilah could see his eyes light up when he realised it was her.

"I will pick you up later?" asked Aunt Mildred. "Or will you bring her back?"

"I will bring her back," smiled Isaiah. "Thank you."

"I am so glad everything has worked out," Aunt Mildred said. Then she turned and drove off.

They looked at each other shyly. He took her hand, and led her up onto the veranda. They sat down, staring out over the farm.

Delilah kept sneaking glances at him. She simply couldn't believe that he was here, and that everything had worked out, in the end.

Isaiah couldn't stop staring at her, either.

"Where is Jeremiah?" she whispered.

"At the police station," he said. "Giving another statement. I'm sorry, Delilah. I thought I was doing the right thing, protecting him. But I shouldn't have done it." He sighed, deeply. "But it wasn't deliberate. Jeremiah pushed Samuel, but he didn't intend what happened. I know that."

Delilah frowned, thinking of the dark cloud that surrounded Jeremiah, but she kept her thoughts to herself.

"Samuel is going to be fine," she said, instead, focusing on the good news. "Apparently, he is going to make a full recovery."

"Praise the Lord," said Isaiah. He looked like he was going to break down, again. "What about us, Delilah? Will you be willing to marry a man who has been charged with attempted murder?"

Delilah looked at him, filled with love. "No," she said. He looked devastated. She smiled. "Not a man charged with attempted murder. But I would be willing to marry a man who is so loyal to his brother, he will do anything to protect him." She paused. "Even if that loyalty was misguided."

Isaiah stood up, pulling her up with him. "What about Katura? Does she understand?"

"Jah," answered Delilah. "We spoke of it the other night. She is happy for the both of us."

"Then everything is how it should be," Isaiah breathed. "We can start over. What about that date on Saturday night?"

Delilah burst out laughing. "Why not?" she answered.

They walked down the veranda steps, laughing and talking. Delilah reflected that it had certainly been a summer to remember, so far. A crime, a jilted cousin, and a marriage proposal.

What on earth would the rest of the summer bring? She would leave that in the hands of the Lord. He seemed to make everything good, in the end.

THE END

LOVINA'S HEART

DEIDRA SCOTT

Chapter One

Lovina Miller took a deep breath as she reached up to pull a piece of laundry from the clothesline and put it in the basket at her feet. Above her head, a pair of bluebirds danced through the bright June sky, reminding her that summer was quickly approaching.

Summer. It was a time full of fresh starts and new beginnings.

Looking across the yard, Lovina watched David Yoder working with one of her brothers. Together, the two young men were struggling with their task, trying to break her *daed's* new horse.

Ach, just watching David sent a thrill of excitement through Lovina's heart. Although she had known him most of her life, there was something about him that could still put a spark inside of her, giving her the feeling that they had just met.

Growing up, Lovina had always dreamed of marrying David. It had just seemed natural to her. With their two houses located side-by-side, they had spent all of their childhood hours playing together in the creek that wound between their properties and climbing the big apple tree like little monkeys.

Lovina had decided early on that she and David would grow old together, spending their adult days raising babies and making a life within their Amish community.

Now that Lovina had turned eighteen-years-old, she felt like she was stuck in the midst of a waiting game, simply counting down the hours until David came forward to begin their relationship together.

Smiling to herself, Lovina basked in the realization that, as an adult, it was now time to watch her childhood dreams start to unfold.

"*Danki* for the help, David!" Lovina heard her father call out from the barn and looked up in time to see David waving goodbye to her family as he started across the yard.

Lovina felt her heart go aflutter when, rather than take the path back to his own parents' house, David veered closer to her own home and made a bee-line right for the clothesline where she was working.

"*Gut* afternoon, David!" Lovina called out, her voice seeming somewhat weak to her own ears.

Watching him come closer, Lovina couldn't help but marvel at how handsome her childhood friend had become. With a head-full of dark red hair and sparkling blue eyes, David had always looked like a cheerful storybook character; however, as he aged, he grew tall and muscular, his boyish looks transforming into that of a good-looking man.

"Hello there, Lovina," David called back, rolling down his sleeves as he walked along, "I tell you, that horse of your *daed's* nearly got me down this time!"

Lovina smiled as she pulled a pair of her brother's pants off of the laundry line and tossed them in the basket, "I guess we should consider ourselves glad to have such a good horse-breaker living so near-by."

To her surprise, David's face suddenly seemed to darken. Taking a deep breath, he reached up and put one hand on the clothesline, "Actually, Lovina, I wanted to talk to you about that."

Although Lovina had hoped that David would want to talk to her alone, she could already tell that his news wasn't going to be what she had wanted to hear.

"Lovina," David looked out across the fields, "Ever since you had your birthday, I'd been hoping..." his voice trailed off and he gave a shrug, "Well, nothing I'd hoped for is going to work out this summer." Standing up taller, he announced, "My uncle from Indiana wrote telling about the need for a good horse-trainer in his community. I agreed to go help for the next three months...I'll be home in time to help my dad get started on the harvest."

Lovina felt her heart drop in her chest. The idea that David would leave had never entered her mind. Even though it was only for three months, it felt like it might as well be three years.

"*Ach*, Lovina, don't be so sad," David reached out and placed his hand on her arm, "I'll be back – I promise. Kentucky is my home...I sure don't have any plans to run off for good."

Something about having his hand on her arm made the pain a little more bearable. Looking up, Lovina met David's tender gaze with her own.

"When I come back..." David took a deep breath and kicked at a clump of grass with his foot. It was strange to see him so uncomfortable – David was usually one to be bold and daring, willing to say whatever was necessary.

"When I come back, I hope we can spend more time together," David managed to say, "Seems like we've grown apart over the years, and I'm ready for that to end."

Lovina couldn't stop the smile that spread across her face, "And maybe not be climbing trees this time?" She added.

David laughed, "Of course we'll be climbing trees again!" He teased.

Growing more sober, he lifted his hand and ran it gently across her cheek, "I'll see you in three months, 'Vina."

Three months. As she watched him walk away and back to his parents' farm across the creek, Lovina took a deep breath and tried to still her thumping heart. Three months was a long time – she was just glad that she had those tender moments to cling to during the summer that stretched out before her.

Chapter Two

Taking a deep breath, David watched out the passenger window as the driver he had hired took him farther and farther from his home in Kentucky and on toward his Uncle Amos' house in Indiana.

"Are you nervous about leaving home for so long?" David's paid driver, Mr. Simpson asked, as he flipped his turn signal on and proceeded toward Uncle Amos' house.

David shook his head and laughed, "*Ach*, no, not nervous."

"Anxious to get away from your parents?" Mr. Simpson asked with a chuckle.

"No, nothing like that." David assured him, "Just glad to be helping my uncle and the people in his community."

Leaning his head back against the headrest of the seat, David closed his eyes and thought about Mr. Simpson's question.

Was he glad to be getting away from his parents? Although he had been quick to assure his driver that wasn't he case, David wasn't so certain himself. To be completely honest, David wasn't a bit sorry to be leaving for the summer. While he had always loved his home and his family, David relished the chance to get away.

Since David had been a little boy, he had always known what was expected of him. He was going to settle down, buy a piece of property close to his parents, and marry Lovina Miller. It wasn't a bad plan at all, but it seemed so boring and dull. Deep in his heart, David had always dreamed of excitement and adventure. Maybe his trip to Indiana would finally provide him with a chance to enjoy his freedom before he settled down for good.

David's driver took him straight to Uncle Amos' house, helped him unload his bags, and then left him to head back to Kentucky.

Uncle Amos and his entire family were happy to welcome David to their home. Uncle Amos explained that everyone in the community could use his horse breaking services and that they would be bringing their horses to his house so that David could train them. Uncle Amos also said that, during David's spare time he could help the family out in the dry goods store they had located in a small shed next to the road.

"I'll take you out to the store now, so that I can show you what kind of work you can do out there." Uncle Amos suggested once David had put his clothes away in the spare bedroom.

Leading David across the yard, Uncle Amos explained, "Of course, I will pay you for helping in the store...and you can also have all the money for training the horses."

David shook his head, "*Ach,* that's too much, Uncle Amos. I'm happy to have the chance to help out."

Uncle Amos chuckled and reached out to give David a slap on the back, "Now, now, don't go talking like that. I'm sure a handsome young man like you should be saving back to buy a nice farm and making plans for the future. I'd dare say that some pretty girl back home has caught your eye."

David gave a shrug, not too anxious to think about his future, "Nothing set in stone just yet."

The graveled lane ended and the two men found themselves standing side-by-side outside of the dry goods store. Reaching out, Uncle Amos pushed the door open, revealing a building with shelves full of baking supplies, canned goods, and some craft items.

"Hannah!" Uncle Amos called out, as he led David through the small building, "Hannah!"

"I'm over here," a soft voice returned.

Turning the corner around one of the shelves, they found a young Amish woman on her knees, busy stacking bags of flour.

"Hannah, I want you to meet my nephew, David," Uncle Amos announced, "David, this is Hannah – she is my wife's cousin and she's helping us out in the store this summer."

Hannah pulled herself to her feet and turned to stare up at David with large, blue eyes. Wisps of dark hair had escaped her prayer *kapp*, making a sort of halo around her face.

Just looking at her, David felt his heart give a leap. She was so unexpectedly beautiful in a dark, mysterious way.

"*Gut* to meet you, David," Hannah replied timidly.

"David is likely to be helping out in the store when he isn't working with the horses," Uncle Amos explained. Giving David a pat on the arm, he motioned toward the back room, "Come on, I want to show you where I store the bulk supplies."

As David followed his uncle, he had a hard time even listening to what was being said. His mind was still mesmerized by the beautiful and timid young lady he had just met. David could hardly wait to get to know and learn more about Hannah.

Lovina sat on the edge of her bed, looking out across the fields of farmland through her bedroom window. Knowing that David was no longer in the house next-door left a hollow emptiness in Lovina's heart. In her eighteen-years, she had never gone a summer without seeing David.

Lovina tired to imagine what her sweet friend was doing at that moment. Did he realize how much she was thinking of him? Did he miss her at all?

Lovina closed her eyes and took a deep breath, "Dear God," she whispered into the darkness, "Please, bring the man that I love back to me."

Chapter Three

David carefully guided his uncle's buggy down the road. It was only his second day in Indiana and work was already starting to pick up; however, Uncle Amos had sent him to town to pick up some nails for a woodworking project he was doing in the barn.

The summer afternoon sun shone down on David and the warmth of the breeze put a smile on his face. David was enjoying his time away from home and, although he had not had many opportunities to spend time with Hannah, he had hopes that would change eventually.

The buggy suddenly took a lung, pulling David out of his thoughts.

"Woah, boy! Woah!" David pulled tightly on the reigns, unsure of what was happening to the buggy. Carefully guiding the horse to the side of the road, he jumped down from his seat and looked over the situation.

Something was wrong with the front buggy wheel. Grabbing a hold of it, David gave it a wiggle, trying to determine if it could keep going.

Pulling off his straw hat, David slapped it against his leg in frustration. He couldn't get to town on that wheel and he didn't think he could make it back to his uncle's house either.

The clipping of oncoming horse hooves made David stand up straighter and wave desperately at the approaching buggy.

The driver was a single Amish man. As soon as David caught his attention, the other driver pulled his buggy to the side of the road behind David.

"Hi there!" David greeted with a smile as he watched the other Amish man get off his buggy and start toward him, "Boy, I sure am glad to see you!" Sticking out a hand, he announced, "I'm David Yoder. I'm staying with my Uncle Amos Yoder – you probably know him."

The stranger nodded and simply said, "I'm Luke Christner." Taking a deep breath, he walked over to the buggy and squatted down to inspect the wheel.

"Looks like this is busted good," he announced, pushing his hat back on his head and reaching up to wipe some sweat from his brow.

David groaned, "I was afraid of that."

Standing to his feet, Luke continued, "I'm afraid you shouldn't drive it any farther than just a few feet or you'll end up wrecking or destroying your entire buggy." With a slight smirk, Luke added, "Lucky for you, this is my parents' drive right up ahead. And I just happen to work on buggies for a living."

David's eyes got large and he let out a huge sigh, "Oh, *gut*! Do you think that you could help me out?"

Luke nodded, "Sure thing. Just lead your buggy down to my workshop. I'll have her fixed up in just a bit."

True to his word, Luke had the buggy wheel fixed within an hour.

David stayed by the young man who had rescued him and worked to fill him in on all the details about his life, his home, and his family. Luke, who seemed to be more reserved, was happy to listen and donate very few details of his own.

"How much do I owe you?" David asked as Luke put the repaired wheel back on his buggy.

Luke gave a shrug as he secured the wheel in place, "Nothing. Consider it a welcome present. Maybe you can help me with one of my horses one day this summer."

"*Ach*," David raised an eyebrow, "I can't let you do that. I took some time you could have been working on other projects..."

Before he could finished, Luke started shaking his head, "No, no you didn't," he assured David as he stood up straight, "Honestly, I didn't have any other work for today." Sighing deeply, he announced, "As badly as we need a horse trainer in this area, we do not need any kind of buggy work. Jobs around here are scarce, David. I was glad to help."

David pondered Luke's statement for a moment. As an idea entered his mind, a broad smile spread across his face, "Listen, Luke! You may not be needed here, but you sure would be in my community! How would you feel about going to Kentucky to spend the summer with my family? It would sure help them out while I'm gone, and you could earn money doing buggy repairs and carpentry work!"

Luke was silent, obviously studying David's suggestion. Finally, with a shrug, he announced, "*Jah* – I don't see why that wouldn't be great. *Danki*, David."

The entire plan made David's face light up like that of a little boy. Grinning from ear-to-ear, he grabbed his new friend's hand in a shake and started making plans to get Luke back to Kentucky.

Chapter Four

Lovina reached up to wipe some sweat from her forehead as she took a break from chopping weeds out of the row of green beans. Despite all her hard work, the weeds were quickly starting to overtake the plants.

David had now been gone two weeks, and Lovina had yet to hear anything from him. His absence made her sad and she wished for all she was worth that she would receive a letter.

Glancing across the field toward his house, she thought of all the times they had snuck away from their chores and played together instead.

To her surprise, Lovina saw a young man approaching her. Could it be…? Lovina's heart dropped as he drew closer. Although she had hoped that it was David, she instantly realized that her eyes had been playing tricks on her. This stranger was even taller than her dear childhood friend and slightly thinner.

"Hullo," Lovina called out as he continued to draw closer.

"Hullo," the stranger returned, his voice deep and almost mysterious, "Are you Lovina Miller?"

Lovina stood up straighter and adjusted her prayer *kapp*, "That would be me. Do I know you?"

The stranger shook his head, "No, you don't." Now he was so close that Lovina was able to get a good look at him. This strange Amish man looked to be in his early twenties, but he seemed more mature. His brown hair was so dark it was almost black, and his eyes a dark color chocolate. Just looking at him made Lovina take a deep breath of surprise. *Ach*, it was hard to remember a time that she had ever seen such a *gut*-looking man!

"I'm Luke Christner. I know your friend, David, and I'm staying with his family until he returns." Glancing toward her house, Luke asked, "Is your *daed* at home? The Yoders told me that he has a construction crew and I'd like a job."

Lovina felt so out of sorts, she wasn't sure what to do. Looking down at her bare feet, she tried to gather her composure. Taking a deep breath, she said, "*Nee*, my *daed* isn't home from work yet, but we're expecting him any minute. If you'd like to wait in the house, my *mamm* can give you some fresh lemonade and cookies."

Luke glanced from the house back to Lovina and then shrugged, "If you don't mind, I'll just stay out here. Looks like you could use some help." Grabbing for an extra hoe, Luke set to work, removing the pesky weeds from among the rows of bean plants.

There was something about Luke that made Lovina feel uncertain about everything. He was a good help in the garden, but she certainly would have felt more at-ease without him. On the other hand, she dreaded him leaving once her father got home from work. Just being near him made her feel things that she had never experienced – she found herself overwhelmed by a sort of giddiness that sprung up from deep within. Although Lovina had always been a talker, she suddenly seemed almost speechless.

"You don't have to do this," Lovina assured him.

Luke simply set his jaw and turned to look at her with his brooding, dark eyes, "I don't have to...but I want to."

Lovina felt weak in the knees, as if she might keel right over. Taking a deep breath, she tried to stead herself.

Suddenly, she found herself a little glad that David was going to be gone for the summer. As quickly as the thought flitted through her mind, she pushed it away; however, just the realization that she could think such a thing left Lovina questioning everything about the future.

David washed his hands in a pail of water that had been set out by the barn, preparing himself for the evening meal. Inside the house, Aunt Miriam was putting the finishing touches on a pot of homemade chili with the help of three of David's cousins.

True to Uncle Amos' word, in the time that David had spent in Indiana he had already been so busy, he hardly had time to even think about being at home.

Wiping his clean hands on a towel, David glanced across the acres of land that his uncle owned. There, in the glowing darkness of the evening, he could make out the form of a young woman walking near the pond.

Hannah.

David had learned to recognize her from a distance. Even though it would be hard to distinguish her from any other Amish woman from so far away, David could pick Hannah out because she was always alone. It seemed like she carried an air of sadness with her, wherever she went.

Taking a deep breath, David stepped out of the barn and started the short walk to the pond.

"Hi there," David called out as he drew near to Hannah.

The young woman looked up at him and gave a sad smile.

"What are you doing?"

Hannah gave a shrug and pulled her black shawl tighter against her shoulders, "I just felt like a walk," she explained.

David stepped up next to her side, "It must be sort of lonely to walk all alone."

Hannah shrugged again, "I'm used to being alone."

David *thought* over his childhood and how little time he had ever spent just to himself. There were always siblings to play with, other Amish children to enjoy at events, and Lovina. Lovina had always been there for him.

Just the thought of his old friend's name sent a nagging sense of guilt through his mind.

Hadn't he promised Lovina that, when he got home, things would be different? Hadn't he promised that they would spend time together? So, what was he doing, trying to get closer to Hannah?

"David..." Hannah's soft voice brought him out of his thoughts, "Are you all right, David? I've never seen you so solemn and quiet."

David looked up at her in surprise, his face breaking out in a broad grin, "Oh, *jah*, I'm fine. I was just thinking is all."

"I didn't know you were able to do that...you know, think without saying what was going through your mind." Although Hannah's words were haughty, David *looked* up in time to catch a teasing smile cross her lips. It was the first time he had ever seen her smile and, something about it made him want to see it a thousand times more.

"Maybe it's too much time around you," David suggested, "Because I don't think you ever say anything much at all."

Hannah's tender smirk turned into a broad smile and David was, once again, captivated by her charm.

Reaching out, he gently took her elbow in his hand, "Would you do me the honor of letting me walk with ya tonight?"

Hannah was silent for a moment, studying David for all that he was worth. Finally, she nodded slowly and said, "*Jah* – I suppose that might be nice."

Chapter Five

Just as David had predicted, it was easy for Luke to find work in Kentucky. He not only spent his afternoons working on buggies in the Yoder's empty shed, but also joined the carpentry work crew lead by Lovina's father.

Lovina wasn't exactly sure how it happened, but it seemed that she and Luke were constantly thrown in the paths of one another. Lovina tried to convince herself that it was merely a coincidence, but she had to admit that it was more than that.

The longer David was gone, the less she was thinking about him and the more she was thinking about Luke.

When he wasn't busy with work, Luke frequently dropped by to help Lovina in the garden; although he wasn't a talker, there was something about his calm attitude that left Lovina yearning for more time with him.

One evening, Lovina baked a plate of her famous homemade ginger snap cookies and decided to take a few across the creek as a thank you for Luke's help in the garden.

Knocking on the shed door, she cautiously pushed it open, cheerfully announcing, "Hello! Luke! Are ya in here?"

"*Jah*, I'm here," Luke replied.

There he was, standing next to a work bench with a busted buggy wheel laid out in front of him.

"Hi there!" Lovina greeted him, suddenly feeling unsure of herself and terribly bashful, "I thought I might bring you something." Placing the plate of cookies on the work table, she watched Luke eyeball them before picking one up and putting it in his mouth.

"It's just a thank you for all the help you've been giving me," she explained.

Luke raised his eyebrows and nodded as he swallowed, "*Danki* – they're very good. You're a good baker, Lovina."

Lovina felt her heart skip a beat with his compliment. Looking at the work he was doing, she added, "Looks like you've got quite a few talents of your own."

Reaching for another cookie, Luke gave a shrug, "I keep busy for sure....but that's a good thing. I'm always thankful for the money."

Leaning back against the table, Lovina studied him in the growing darkness, "Saving back for a farm of your own?"

Luke stared straight at his work and shook his head, "No. I'm going to give my money to help out my family. I have no need of a place of my own."

"Don't you ever hope to get married and have a family?"

Luke shook his head slowly, "I'm afraid all of my dreams are gone. I plan to be alone forever."

His words broke Lovina's heart. Although he tried to sound resolved, it was easy to hear the pain in his voice.

"*Ach*, Luke," she managed to whisper with a smile, "Don't say that. You never know what might happen."

Luke took in a deep breath and then let it out slowly. Looking up to meet Lovina's eyes, he studied her for what seemed minutes before asking, "What about you? Do you think that you could ever love someone like me?"

His question took Lovina by such surprise that she almost fell over. Her eyes growing large, she looked down at the floor, her heart flooded by a million different emotions.

"I...I...Luke..." Lovina's voice was trailing in every direction but her words were making no sense at all.

"Lovina," Reaching out, Luke put his hand on top of hers, "Would you consider going with me to the singing after church this weekend?"

It felt like Lovina would not be able to breath, so many decisions were running helter-skelter through her mind. Almost a surprise to herself, she heard her voice say, "Sure. I don't see why not."

Although David had been staying busy with the horses, he still managed to make some time to help out in the store. With a beautiful girl like Hannah there, he had to find time to spend with her.

One afternoon they had received a large order of supplies and were hurrying to put them on the shelves before it would be too dark to see, even by the glow of the lantern.

"*Ach*, this is a job!" David grumbled as he hurried to put some bags of flour in their place on a shelf, "Of course this would just happen to be the night that Uncle Amos and his entire family went visiting...leaving you and me to do all the work."

Hannah smiled and shook her head, "David, you complain so much. I don't mind the work. Work keeps me busy...work keeps my mind off of...other things."

Suddenly interested, David looked up in surprise. Maybe he would finally have a chance to hear some of the secrets that were hidden away behind this mysterious girl's sad blue eyes.

"What other things?" David asked.

Hannah shrugged as she ran her fingers over a bag of sugar, "Disappointments...heartbreaks...bad decisions."

Hannah went silent, assuring David that he would hear no more of her story, but then she surprised him when she went on to clear her throat and say, "I had a boyfriend...a fiancé even."

As the words came pouring out of her mouth, it was easy to see that they were tearing her apart. Hannah closed her eyes and continued, "But things didn't work out. We were engaged but...well, I was filled with so many uncertainties. I called off the wedding before it was even announced in church. I didn't mean to end everything with him – I just needed more time to think. But I'm afraid he took it as an outright rejection. And now, I'll never have a chance with him again," Hannah reached up to wipe away the tears that were threatening to overwhelm her, "*Ach*, David, it almost breaks my heart to talk about it. I have destroyed all my chances for happiness."

Looking at her in the light of the lantern, her face clouded over with pain and tears gathering in her eyes, David felt totally broken for her. Pulling himself to his feet, he stood up straight and stepped closer to her, putting a hand on her thin shoulder.

"Hannah," he whispered her name with all the tenderness that he had been storing in his heart, "Dear Hannah...you still have a thousand chances for happiness." Reaching up, he took his thumb and brushed a tear off of her cheek.

Hannah took a deep breath and let it out slowly. Looking at him in surprise, she simply whispered, "*Danki*, David." Then she squared her shoulders and announced, "Let's get back to work."

Chapter Six

Over the next few days, David and Hannah had little time to spend together. He looked forward to ever chance he had to see her. Although their friendship had not had time to progress, David felt confident that over the rest of the summer he could easily earn himself a special place in Hannah's lonely heart.

One afternoon, David had finally found a chance to work in the dry goods store alongside Hannah when one of his cousins came rushing into the shed with a letter in his outstretched hand.

"David," the little cousin called out, "You got some mail!"

Taking the letter, David quickly recognized the handwriting as that of his younger sister, Lydia.

Ripping the seal open, David pulled out the letter, unsure why his teenage sister would even take the time to write him.

Dear David,

I don't want to bother you while you're gone, but I need to let you know something important. I've always thought that you and Lovina had something special together, although I'm not sure if you had any kind of plans for the future or an agreement. While you've been gone, Lovina has taken a spark to the very man you sent here to work – Luke Christner. Seems like they're seeing each other almost every day and last night I overheard him invite her to the singing Sunday night. She agreed to go with him.

I don't mean to stick my nose in where it doesn't belong, but I know that you were always sweet on Lovina and just thought you should know.

Your sister,

Lydia

"*Ach*," David read over the letter and then reread it again, his heart suddenly dropping into his stomach.

Lovina – with Luke? A multitude of emotions suddenly assailed David. He found himself so frustrated, almost angry at Luke for stealing his girl. How dare Luke go to David's own home and try to take the woman he loved away from him? David was hurt, so hurt, by Lovina's decision to move forward with a relationship with someone else. But, worst of all, David felt incredible guilt and sadness.

Deep in his heart, David realized that it was his own fault that Lovina and Luke were growing close. In all the time that David had been in Indiana, he had never taken the time to even write his childhood sweetheart a letter – he had just always taken for granted that she would be there for him when he returned.

While he had been busy pursing a friendship with Hannah, he had never thought that Lovina might be looking at someone else.

Reaching up, David rubbed his hand across his face, trying to gather his wits and decide what to do next.

"What is wrong, David?" Hannah asked softly as she stepped up next to him.

David balled his free hand up into a fist, fighting the urge to destroy the letter he had just received. Passing it to Hannah, he quickly explained, "I don't know how to tell you this, Hannah, but Lovina...well, she and I have always been friends. I don't mean to have led you astray in any way because I have liked you since the day we met but this..." David couldn't go on.

Hannah took the letter in her own hands and read it slowly, her eyes growing large as she went over the message again and again.

"David," she managed to breath softly, "What are you going to do?"

David brushed his hand through his hair as memories of Lovina ran across his mind, "I don't know. I just don't know." Turning, he gave the floor a hard kick with the toe of his boot.

"David," Hannah took a deep breath and shook her head slowly, "I hate to say this, but you know that we aren't meant to be together. No matter how happy we might have both been to pretend...it just isn't so. You have made my summer much more enjoyable...but it's time to get back to our real lives."

David looked down at his feet. He wanted to fight her words; he hated the idea of giving Hannah up completely. But, when he thought of his dear Lovina...he knew that he couldn't live without her.

"Go to her, David!" Hannah exclaimed, "Go to Lovina and let her know that you love her."

Taking a deep breath, David nodded his head, "I'll go call a driver right now."

Chapter Seven

David sat in the passenger seat of the truck, half-heartedly listening as his driver talked incessantly during the long trip back home. Looking out the window, David watched the scenery slowly change from the flat Amish country of Indiana to the rolling hills of Kentucky.

With each mile that passed, it seemed that David got even more nervous about his future with Lovina.

When he first started home, he had been certain that she would be glad to see him but now...well, the closer he got to her, the less sure he became. Maybe she had truly fallen for Luke and she wouldn't want to even see him. Maybe David had blown his one and only chance for true love with the only girl he ever truly cared for.

Lovina had just filled up a bucket of water and got down on her knees to scrub the kitchen floor with a scrub brush when she heard a truck pull up in the front yard.

Ach, Lovina thought to herself as she plunged her hands down into the soapy water, *Daed must have visitors.*

It was Saturday afternoon and Lovina found her mind plagued with thoughts of Luke and their upcoming date. Although she truly enjoyed spending time with him, there was something about agreeing to go on a date with him that put her mind entirely in a tizzy. As much as she liked Luke and was attracted to him, Lovina battled thoughts of David – it seemed so sad to be turning her back on their relationship with each other.

But, she reasoned to herself, when she thought back on it, she and David had never had a true relationship. Sure, he had always been a good friend to her, but it seemed that was all things were to ever be. Since he left for Indiana, she had not heard a word from him and, as sad as she was to admit it, she was starting to wonder if he would ever come home at all.

"Lovina."

The voice seemed to come out of no where. Lovina looked up in surprise, wondering if she was truly hearing a person or if it was her own imagination.

There, standing in the doorway to the kitchen, was David himself.

"David!" Lovina managed to breathe as she struggled to pull herself to her feet, "Oh, David...is that really you?"

In an instant, David had bridged the space between them. He came right to her side, nearly knocking her bucket of soapy water over in his hurry.

"Lovina," David managed to say, somewhat louder this time, "Lovina..." he seemed to want to say more, but acted as if he couldn't find the words. Reaching out, he grabbed Lovina and gathered her into his arms.

To Lovina, everything felt like a crazy dream. Pressed firmly against her old friend's body, all thoughts of Luke vanished from her mind as she let David hold her like a little girl.

"Lovina," David pulled back only long enough to kiss her on the mouth, "Lovina, I have been a total moron. I am so sorry!"

"David," Lovina managed to say as she tried to catch her breath, "David...what has happened?"

David stepped back as he struggled to gather his composure. Reaching up, he wiped away at tears that threatened to overtake him.

"Lovina," he reached out and held her hands in his own, "I have been so ignorant. I left home, anxious to find adventure and experience new things...and I almost lost the one thing that means the most to me in the world – you."

Lovina felt her heart start to melt as David poured out his soul to her, "Lovina, I love you. I love you more than I ever realized. I thought that Uncle Amos was giving me a chance to experience adventure but I think it was actually the good Lord allowing me the opportunity to realize how much I love you. Please, Lovina...I don't want to wait any longer. Say that you will marry me!"

There had never been anything that Lovina wanted more. In that instant, it felt like all of her hopes and dreams were finally coming true.

Luke.

The name entered her mind suddenly and it felt like the life was drained right out of her. Oh, but hadn't she already led him to believe that she cared for him? Hadn't she already agreed to go out on a date with him this very weekend?

"David," Lovina squeezed her dear friend's hands tightly as she looked for the right words to share her news, "David. I have been a foolish girl."

"And I have been a foolish man," David was quick to add.

Lovina smiled and shook her head, "Perhaps we've both been foolish..."

Her words were cut short as the sound of an approaching vehicle brought them both from their thoughts.

Glancing out the window, they watched together as a strange car stopped in front of the house and let out a passenger.

David felt his heart sink when he saw the visitor who was getting out of the strange car.

It was Hannah.

David thought that she had understood. What was she doing...following him all the way to Kentucky of all places? Hadn't she been the one who had said that their relationship wasn't going to work and even pushed him to return to Lovina? What was she doing here now?

David battled the urge to run forward and stop her before she could get to the house. Turning to Lovina, he struggled to find the words to explain what was surely about to come.

"Lovina..." he hurried to say, "While I was gone, I was an idiot. I hate telling you this more than you will ever know, but I got involved with a girl from Indiana. We never started to court, but we were heading in that direction when I heard that you and Luke had begun a relationship...."

As the words poured from his mouth, David watched Lovina's face turn ashen and then red with shame.

"You already know about Luke?" She managed to whisper.

David nodded his head, "That was the wake-up call I needed. That was what I needed to bring me back home. I never want to risk losing you again, Lovina!"

Lovina started to wipe tears away from her eyes, "David, I don't want to lose you either! But what you heard is true. Luke and I have grown close and are on the verge of starting a relationship. I was so foolish, David, but I was afraid I had lost you and now I don't know what to do..."

In the other room, they could hear a knock on the front door.

Wiping at her eyes, Lovina hurried to go open it with David trailing close behind. When she opened the door, Hannah was standing on the front porch, a determined look in her blue eyes.

"I need to talk to David," she announced, looking from Lovina to David.

"David," she took a deep breath, "I need to go to your house...I need to see Luke."

Luke? David was more confused than ever. Cocking his head to one side, he tried to understand where this strange twist came into play.

"You don't have to look far," the deep voice of Luke spoke out and they all turned in surprise to find that he had come up on the porch and was standing just out of view.

"Hannah," as he said the name, his voice seemed to fill with a strange sort of pain.

"*Ach*, Luke..." Hannah looked down at her black shoes as if she couldn't hold his gaze, "I have been wanting to talk to you."

Luke shook his head sadly, "I can't imagine what we would have to say to each other now."

"Luke...you know that I am a very shy girl," Hannah said in a shaky voice, "And I have let my fear get the better of me far too many times. I almost let it destroy what we had together. But Luke...I can't let that happen."

David's eyes got large as he realized that Luke must be the ex-beau that Hannah had told him about.

"I love you, Luke," Hannah announced resolutely, "I love you and I still want to be your wife...if you can ever find it in your heart to have me."

David watched Luke and held his breath, hoping that he would agree.

Stepping forward, Luke reached out and took Hannah in his arms, "I love you too, Hannah!" He exclaimed as he cupped her face in his hands, "I have always loved you and I always will." Turning to look at Lovina, he quickly tried to explain, "Lovina, I hope that you understand..."

Lovina smiled broadly as she wrapped her arms around David's waist, "It is fine, Luke. I think that things are exactly the way that they are supposed to be!"

Epilogue

Standing together at the kitchen sink, Lovina and David watched as a group of children played outside in their front yard.

"Look at those crazy things," Lovina muttered as she noticed her daughter trying to climb a tree.

"Just like us when we were little," David announced.

Lovina looked up at him and smirked, "*Jah* – and I think our little girl might have a crush on the neighbor boy, as well."

David and Lovina had now been married for ten years and had three children of their own. It had been a double wedding shared with Hannah and Luke, who decided to move to Kentucky so that Luke would continue to enjoy a steady stream of work.

David and Lovina had built their house behind his parents' place and, to their surprise, Hannah and Luke had bought a piece of farm land right across the creek.

Their children played together and it wouldn't be any surprise if someday those same children would grow up to marry one another.

David smiled broadly and gathered his wife up in his arms.

"I'm glad I went to Indiana that summer," he announced as he reached out to push a strand of her brown hair back from her face, "Because that summer showed me how much I need you in my life."

Bending over, he gave her a gentle kiss.

Life truly was as David and Lovina had always imagined it – and they were happier than they ever could have guessed possible.

THE END

The Amish Promise

MEGHAN MASON

Nothing could have created a more romantic and joyful afternoon, as David and Rachael sat upon the checked picnic blanket. David had been planning this occasion for months now, and he had put very careful preparations into what was hopefully going to prove to be the happiest days of their lives. David had fallen in love with Rachael from the beginning, when they first met at the Amish community fall social. Very soon after, he knew that she was exactly perfect for him in every way possible. He wanted her to be his wife, and to build a family together. Because of this happy realization, David had been making plans about how and when to pop the important question. He had secretly already asked her father, Abel, for his daughter's hand in marriage, and Abel had been pleased to hear of David's intentions. He knew David to be a very hardworking young man who respected the traditions of the Amish with much reverence. He could not have chosen a better husband for Rachael if he had tried. David left her father's barn that day, his heart bursting with pride and happiness. Now his biggest responsibility was to create the perfect atmosphere to ask his beloved to marry him.

It had taken David just two weeks to imagine the plan, and put it into action! He wanted something simple, so he opted for a lovely picnic lunch in the meadow of his parents' farm. It was situated nicely in the back of the property, and was filled with large, mature oak trees, wildflowers in full bloom, and warm yet breezy weather. He enlisted the help of his eldest sister, Gloria, to assist him in making a light lunch. She had prepared sandwiches, fresh fruit, and homemade apple cider, and packed it all away in a wicker picnic basket. David selected a soft blanket, and went off to pick up Rachael, for what she thought to be a simple date in the fresh air.

Once there, David laid out blanket his grandmother had made years ago, and guided Rachael by the hand to sit down for lunch. His heart soared as he admired his true love, and it felt like all Gott's creatures understood what was about to happen. Birds tweeted from their nests, bugs stayed conveniently away, and the few rabbits and squirrels looked on as if excited to see the plan play out. David withdrew a tiny wooden box from his breast pocket, and looked her straight in the eyes,

"Rachael, you must know by now that you are my beloved. I want to ask for you to become my wife," and he opened the box to reveal a simple golden band, "please say yes, and make me the happiest man alive," he declared. Rachael's glistening eyes gleamed in the sunlight, as she gazed at the glint of the beautiful band, and she instantly knew what her answer was to be,

"Yes, David! I thought you'd never ask," she laughed, and he slipped the band onto her finger. They were far too excited to eat any lunch, so they hastily packed up the basket, and returned to the farmhouse. There, as was to be expected, sat his mamm, daed, schwesters and bruders,

"What is this now?" asked his daed, "back so early from the meadow?"

"Yes, father! Rachael had said yes to my proposal, though we were too excited to even eat," and he looked at Gloria to make sure he had not inadvertently hurt her feelings. Gloria giggled, and exclaimed in Pennsylvania Dutch,

"Nau is awwer bsll Zert!" which translated into English as *'Now it's about time!'* Everyone congratulated the young couple, and the basket was re-opened to share amongst the family. Gloria had made lots of extra anyway, so it turned into quite a nice family gathering.

It was beginning to darken as the evening set in, and David drove Rachael back to her home in the buggy. They said their goodbyes, and promised to meet soon, after the big harvest. All the men, including her own father and bruders would be working hard to harvest all the grain, corn, and other seasonal crops. After that big job, the two would certainly have plenty of time to plan the ceremony. She waved at David, as he steered the old buggy back towards his father's farm.

Rachael told her family all about the amazing afternoon that she had spent with David's family, and showed off the pretty band. It would not be long before they were joined together in matrimony. Her mamm cried, as mamms are prone to do, and ran to get the family wedding dress out of the hope chest in her room. It had been in their family for generations, and her mother was overjoyed that her only daughter was now going to be the special girl to wear the dress. Though made of simple cotton with spots of delicate embroidery, it was such a meaningful family tradition. She began to daydream of perhaps having a granddaughter someday that the dress would be passed on to eventually. Her own sister had never married, and had recently taken ill in an Amish settlement in Indiana, so the dress had passed to Ellen instead. Poor Eliza had had no children of her own, and though she felt sad for her sister, she was happy to be next in line for the dress. The rest of the evening was spent eating a celebratory supper of roast beef, roasted potatoes, and the green beans picked fresh from the garden. It appeared that nothing could ruin the joy of these families that were about to become one!

Early the next morning, while Rachael was picking vegetables from the garden, a stranger in a buggy came rumbling up the drive towards their home. The man removed his hat in polite greeting to Rachael, and went to knock upon the door. Her mamm answered, as the menfolk were out for the harvest work, and the girls were all home keeping up with the household chores. Her mamm seemed to recognize the stranger, and invited him in to the house. Rachael was curious about who the stranger could be. The Amish rarely had unknown visitors outside of the community, so this was slightly intriguing, if not a bit unsettling. If Rachael had only known just how unsettling the stranger's news was to be, she would probably have run off that very minute towards David's family. Her mamm called her in with a grim look about her face, and it was then that her heart sank. She felt an unnerving feeling of unexplainable dread, as she made her way from the garden to the house. Why was this man here, and why had she been beckoned by her mamm? Many anxious questions began to form in her mind, as she plodded carefully with her apron full of vegetables. Mamm took the vegetables, and bade her daughter to sit down at the family table. She did not look happy, and this further worried Rachael,

"Daughter, something dreadful has happened to your aunt Eliza. This is Brant, come all the way from Indiana to explain the details." She looked at her daughter with pity and sadness, but Rachael was still clueless as to how this should involve her. She listened to Brant's words,

"Hello, my dear. I am Brant Williams. I am an old friend of your mamm's family, and I have traveled very far to deliver some saddening news. Your Aunt Eliza's health is now worse than ever, and a family member is needed to come care for her in her dying days." Rachael's face fell at this news, as she barely knew her Aunt Eliza, and had a terrible feeling she was to be that family representative,

"What is it that must be done for auntie?" she said hesitantly.

Her mamm took hold of the situation, and explained,

"Rachael, dear, you are the not the eldest child, as your bruder, Hamm, is over twenty, but as the oldest female, you are expected to go and care for Eliza. I would gladly take your place, but the responsibility falls to you."

"What does this all mean? What will happen now that I am to marry David?" she inquired desperately, "I am to be planning a wedding in two short weeks, mamm!" Her mother's countenance turned stern, and Rachael knew then that she had spoken with selfishness. If this was truly her duty, she was bound to do whatever was necessary for Aunt Eliza. This would undoubtedly mean many months away from home, and from David. She tried in vain to hide her tears, but only could squeak out a few words before fleeing to her bedroom,

"Sorry, Mr. Williams an mamm. I, of course, will go," and she dashed away towards the back of the house. She threw herself pathetically on the bed, and let out all the tears that came with the disappointment of postponing the wedding. All had been so happy the night before, and now it felt like the world was coming to an end. Little did Rachael know what tragic events were about to unfold in her otherwise ordinary, simple, and predictable life in the quaint community of Oakhurst Village.

The following afternoon, Rachael was packed and ready as she ever could manage to be, and Mr. Brant Williams had stayed the night to give Rachael more time to let the news soak in. He had his own family, after all, and knew quite well the sacrifices that were sometimes required. Still, he felt badly for Rachael, knowing the predicament caring for Eliza now meant. Her wedding would be postponed, but he and her parents encouraged her to keep the faith that all would work out in good time. She sent word to David via one of her bruders, and received a reply that wished her well, though expressed his sorrow that they would have to alter their plans. Both knew in their hearts, however, that if someone was in need, it was the right thing to do. Brant hooked up the horses to the rickety looking buggy for their rather long trip to Indiana. They would stop along the way to spend the nights at various Amish villages, and Brant reassured her parents that she would be well taken care of throughout the journey. It was also explained to her that Eliza was in a bad way, close to death, and would require ongoing care until Gott called her home to his heavenly paradise. The doctor would come and assess Eliza once again once Rachael had arrived. It appeared that all was well in hand, and that caring for her aunt would be a good and kind gesture. After all, she was family, and no one should have to suffer alone or so far from family if it could be prevented. She prayed about her new adventure in Indiana, a place she'd never been, and asked Gott to bless Eliza. She could not bear it if she was to suffer in unbearable pain, and was not all that familiar with medical care. Her mamm had given her a book of household remedies, and instructed her to make use of it if needed. She held tightly to the book as if it was the guidebook for caring for the dying, even though Eliza was most likely too far gone to be aided by homemade health recipes. They would have to rely on the doctor's orders, and try to make Aunt Eliza as comfortable as possible. It was also understood that Brant would drop in weekly to deliver groceries and supplies, so that Rachael's full attention could be on her aunt's welfare. Eliza owned a small cottage in the main street of her village. She had many friends, but it being harvest, the women of their houses would be needed at home. Rachael was the best option, and she resolved to do her best with a compassionate and loving heart. She tried to pass the long journey by imagining life as David's wife, and the bopplis they might have one day soon.

After a week's journey, Brant and Rachael arrived in Well's Landing. If she never saw the seat of that old buggy again, it would be too soon. Gingerly, she stepped down as Brant helped her down. He took charge of her modest traveling bag, and they proceeded to call upon Aunt Eliza. There was a friendly nurse assistant currently sitting at her bedside keeping diligent watch. She offered Rachael advice as to how to comfort her ailing relative until Doc Warner could make the drive into the center of town. Apparently, the doctor was to be expected the day after tomorrow, so hopefully Rachael could handle things until then. With a grateful hug, Rachael bid Brant and the nurse assistant goodbye, and began to settle in to her small room beside her aunt's main bedroom. It was a connecting room, with a shared indoor bathroom, so at least there would be that convenience. The nurse had left instructions on when to brew the medicinal tea, and what times to try to feed broth to Eliza. Rachael had to admit that the unfortunate woman whom she barely knew, looked like she had been ravished by disease for some time now. She unpacked her bag, and went off to the kitchen to boil some water.

Doc Warner made his appearance at noon the following day. He took all of Eliza's vital signs, and asked Rachael to please continue the same care for as long as Eliza would last. If her aunt experienced any adverse reactions or serious pain, she was to send word as quickly as possible. He directed her to run next door to the general store where they had a modern phone installed. That way, the doctor would be there in good time with something to ease the pain or increased sickness. Rachael followed him out, thanked him, and paid the bill with the money her mamm had sent for that purpose. She then returned to Eliza's bedside, where her aunt mostly slept. During these lengthy naps, Rachael wrote daily letters home to David, and worked on sewing their wedding quilt. In the evenings, she straightened the tiny house, and prepared broth and tea, in addition to her own small meals. She always had David on her mind, and hoped all was going well back home with the harvesting. She always mentioned in the letters how much she missed her fiancé, and that she hoped that Eliza would not have to endure too much more suffering. It was difficult for Rachael to comfort her when she was awake, as she could never get comfortable. During these lucid times, she read aloud to Aunt Eliza from the bible.

The following week, she received a letter from home, but this time it looked like it had been written in David's mother's hand. She wondered why the letter was addressed in Mrs. Todd's handwriting rather than David's, but she was excited to get the letter nonetheless. She carefully opened the envelope, and perused the contents of the letter. Rachael felt faint as she read the horrible news about David! His mamm reported that during the past week, a terrible accident had befallen her son. During an afternoon of harvesting with his daed and bruders, David had been asked to go fetch some feed from the barn. The feed sacks had been stored up above in the hay loft area. As David climbed the ladder to the loft, the top rung broke in half, causing him to fall to the barn floor. He had broken both legs, and cracked several ribs. The doctor came at once, but David was in serious pain. In addition to the broken bones, he apparently suffered a damaging blow to the head. Upon landing awkwardly on the barn floor, he had hit the side of his head on a large tool box. The head injury was proving to be the most serious of David's injuries, and he had fallen into a state of unconsciousness shortly after the doctor had left. Mrs. Todd went on to explain that they called the doctor back as soon as possible, but that he was rather skeptical that David would awaken given the severity of the fall. He had sustained so many injuries that the family was growing fearful of his recovery. Rachael dropped the letter, and slumped to the floor. How could this be happening? Her David was hurt, and she was so far away. It was heartbreaking news, and she sobbed much of the night. Not only was she going to lose her aunt, but the love of her life was now clinging to life, and she was not able to get frequent updates. A letter per week was all that was coming in, and she continued to cry herself to sleep every night. Every letter conveyed similar news that David was not showing any improvement. He was still deep in a coma, and his schwesters and mamm were keeping a very close eye on him. To make matters worse, poor Aunt Eliza had taken a turn for the worse, and was now becoming delirious, murmuring in her sleep, and raving when she was awake. She phoned Doc Warner, and he prescribed a sedative from the chemist. An errand boy delivered the powder to the door with instructions on how much to administer as well as how often. Doc Warner said the end was near, and that the sedative was likely the only thing that would keep her comfortable. It was hard to tell if she would last hours, days, or even a week. As she watched over her aunt, she prayed for a peaceful passing. She was certain that Gott knew best, and she continued to rely heavily upon her faith to get her through these long days and nights. She prayed daily for David too, fervently begging the Lord to spare him, so that they could continue to have a life together. Even if she had to care for a disabled husband, she would always be devoted to the man she loved.

A few agonizing days later, her aunt's breathing became extremely labored. The doctor was again summoned to the cottage. This time, there was no hope left for Eliza, as the doctor explained how much time was likely left,

"Die sunn is am unnergeh (*the sun is setting*) upon our schwester, Eliza, and we pray Gott to take her into his heavenly kingdom." Then Doc Warner sat in the kitchen along with the undertaker, awaiting the inevitable moment that Eliza's spirit would leave her earthly body. It happened late in the night, and Rachael allowed the men to do what was necessary to prepare Eliza for burial. A sad pall fell upon her as she thought about her aunt's last few months. She hoped against hope that David was not in similar circumstances. At least after the funeral, which the entire community attended, she would make the return trip to Pennsylvania. Brant readied the buggy once more, and off they went so that Rachael could nurse yet another ailing loved one. She was absolutely desperate to reach David's bedside. He needed her, and she needed him, and she continued her unwavering prayers to Gott. This time she felt little discomfort from the bumpy ride in the decrepit buggy, as her thoughts were entirely on David. It had been at least two weeks since she had heard word from the family. This was mostly due to the time it took to travel from Indiana to home, with several stops along the way to stay the nights. She refused to take proper care of herself, until Brant sat her down for a good talking to,

"Rachael, what good will this do for David? You must eat, sleep, and take proper care of yourself. He will need you to be fit as a fiddle, so that you can nurse him back to health!" Although he was completely uncertain whether there was much hope for David or not, he figured the best thing to do was to try to raise the girl's spirits. The last thing anyone needed was another sick person. Rachael was so worn out from caring for Eliza, that Brant was worried that David's condition would do her in for certain if things did not begin to change.

Late in the morning the next day, Brant drove the buggy towards her mamm's house. He helped her down by offering his hand as support, but she seemed weak and brokenhearted. Her mamm ran to greet them, and when Rachael spied her mother, she collapsed in exhaustion into her arms. Brant carried her into her bedroom, as her mamm prepared a meal for them both. He had driven through the night so that Rachael could arrive home as soon as possible. He felt horrified that she had not fared as well as he had hoped. Sometimes a broken heart was just as damaging if not more so than a broken bone. He had learned that when his own mamm had passed away nearly twenty years ago. She had been the backbone of his family, and he had been very close to her. He had to work hard to get back on track, because his family needed him to be strong. He sat with her parents for the next few nights, until she recovered properly. Her mamm's careful attention and loving care proved to be the most healing element besides the power of prayer. When everyone was sure that Rachael was much improved in both body and spirit, he bid the family farewell, and headed back to his village. Meanwhile, her mamm and daed debated over when to get her over to David's side. His condition had not changed since the beginning, and his parents were beginning to lose hope. It was difficult enough to lose a family member, but when it was a child it was a million times more painful. They came to the decision that Gloria would come to fetch her in the morning, and her mamm would pack another traveling bag for her daughter. Now that she was stronger, well-nourished, and back home, Rachael did her best to use all of her strength and faith to help David. She planned to stay by his side no matter the outcome. There was even talk of a symbolic ceremony to wed the two lovers, if the doctor decided there was little chance for regaining consciousness. No one uttered a word of these melancholy plans to Rachael, so everyone in the village continued to offer food and other home comforts that David's family needed. After the accident, his daed stopped the harvest, and it was up to his bruders and family friends to finish the essential work. It was the only way that the Todd's brought in any income, and Mr. Todd was forlorn with grief. He and his wife had the preacher visit every other day, and everyone gathered for a prayer circle. Rachael had brought back with her the finished wedding quilt. As soon as she saw him, she removed the drab blankets, wiped his brow, and wrapped him gently in the quilt. Hopefully, on some level, he could feel her presence and know that she was pouring all her love into caring for his every need. This also gave his parents a much-needed break to rest. They were thankful that she was now safely back home where she was dearly needed.

As she tended to her comatose lover, Rachael did her best to make his surroundings as cheerful as possible. She went out to the meadow, the place where he had proposed, and picked a bunch of wild flowers. She put several vases of sweet smelling buds around his pillows, so that he might sense the pretty aroma of that romantic day. She also spoke to him about the future, and read to him from the bible. She chose passages that spoke of love and how merciful Gott could be to those who clung to their faith. She prayed that these things combined would aid in helping David regain consciousness. She began to hum church hymns close to his ear while holding his hand. She recited possible names for their future children, and invented stories of family outings and special holiday gatherings. She told stories of them becoming grandparents in their later years, with all their grandchildren surrounding them. The Todd's even set up a special cot for her, so that he would always have her next to him. That way, just in case he came to, his intended would be there to greet him.

It was after all these tireless gestures, and long days and nights, that Rachael fell into a deep slumber. She had been singing to David, when she eventually drifted off to sleep with her head resting gently upon his chest. Her arms were folded around his neck in the careful cradle she often used when she sang close to his ear. This is how she fell asleep that night. And, in the morning, quite early just before sunrise, this was the way she awoke to soft whispers coming from David. His eyes were struggling to flutter open, and his hand quivered slightly within her own. She sat up immediately, still grasping his hand, and called out for the Todd's. The entire family gathered in the hallway outside his sickroom. His mamm and daed came into the room to see what the commotion was. David had finally woken up after so long! Rachael fell to his bedside,

"Oh, David! My love! You have returned to us..." and she wept tears of joy. She allowed his parents to have some private time with their son, while she ran to the kitchen with Gloria. They got busy preparing a very simple and plain breakfast of the nourishing foods that the doctor had written down if he came out of the coma. He would be extremely weak in the months to follow, and would have to adhere to strict bedrest for the ribs and legs to mend completely. Rachael made up a tray, complete with a few flowers from the meadow, and quickly shooed everyone away, so that he could eat his breakfast in peace and quiet. He still had quite a long road of recovery before him, and comfort and love were of the utmost importance in keeping his spirits up. He finished his meal the best he could, and gazed at Rachael. He blinked away a few tears, but was not yet able to speak. As David spent the next two months recovering, Rachael was always there to help him. She continued everything that she had been doing while he was in the coma, but added a few soft conversations as his speech was restored to him. She urged him to exercise his limbs that were movable to prevent bedsores and atrophy of his muscles. She helped his mamm and Gloria when he needed bathing, and they allowed her free reign of the kitchen to prepare all his meals. The two ate together in his room until he was strong enough to be wheeled out to the common table. A few farmers had taken up a collection to craft a wheelchair for David, so that he could get around before he was ready for crutches. That way, Rachael could sit with him on the front porch. They breathed in the fresh air, and David's health continued to improve,

"Rachael, tell me again how you came to me? How far did you travel to be at my side?"

"Darling, I was with my Aunt Eliza for some months, and got word from your mother about the accident. Do you remember falling from the ladder in the barn?" she asked.

"No, my memory is so foggy. All I can remember is floating across the sky over the beautiful meadow. I kept looking down to see how I was flying with no wings, and below I saw the two of us just like on that day. I would try to speak to them, to us, but the words would not come out. Then I recall an angelic voice singing songs from church, and it was almost as if it was someone calling me back to reality," recalled David, "it must have been your sweet singing that I was hearing in the distance. It was beckoning me homeward, but I was flying in the opposite direction towards a light."

"It sounds like you hovered between life and death. You were very unstable, and your heart rate was very slow at times. Perhaps all our prayers called you back to where you belong. Gott decided your time here was not yet finished. With my Aunt Eliza, despite our prayers, it was her time to go. Gott knows best when it is our time. But for you, Gott must have given you a purpose here with the people who love you! I always prayed for you, and when I did, I asked Him to spare you, so that we might have a life together. But we must be grateful for the blessings He has given to us. We must give back something special to our community, David. We must show our gratitude for the many gifts Gott has bestowed upon us."

"I agree wholeheartedly, my dear Rachael," continued David, and he seemed to hesitate to say anything more. He appeared sleepy, and it had been a long day. She wheeled him back inside, set out dinner for his family, and got him into bed,

"You need to be careful not to tax yourself too soon, David. Our marriage can wait until you are fully yourself again. I don't care how long it takes. Now lie down, and have pleasant dreams," and she kissed his forehead goodnight. She tucked the marriage quilt snugly around him, and David drifted off to sleep.

Yet another month passed by, and David was steadily gaining strength. His legs had healed, and he got back to walking slowly with a renewed sense of purpose. There was something very important that he had to do without Rachael's knowledge. One morning when Rachael was back at her own home visiting her family, David requested that his daed drive him to the preacher's house in town. He shared his secret with his father, because he knew how happy it would make his parents,

"Daed, I want the preacher to visit this afternoon and perform the wedding ceremony. I want to surprise Rachael. We only need our closest family members there, and a normal family meal. That is what truly matters to me, and I think then Rachael and I will move into the vacant cottage across from the preacher. I have a plan that I would like to run by the preacher, and if he agrees, then it would be best for Rachael and me to be near the center of town."

"What is the plan, David?" his father asked excitedly. But, David being David, he would not give away the idea he had been formulating for some time now.

"All in good time, Daed," and he smiled as they knocked upon the preacher's door. Pastor Robert answered, and invited the two men in to the sitting room. His wife prepared tea, and they sat down to discuss the viability of the ceremony to take place that afternoon, and then David requested to speak to Pastor Robert alone. They spoke only for about thirty minutes, and they rejoined Mr. Todd. Everyone piled into the buggy, and headed towards the Todd Farm. Once there, David shared his secret plans for the ceremony with his mamm and schwesters and bruders. Gloria and his other sister, May, made up some simple decorations of flower garlands, and draped them beautifully across the barn. The barn where the terrible accident had taken place had been completely renovated by the town's menfolk. It was part of the Amish tradition to raise new structures as a group. They had down a spectacular job, and the barn was still pristine. No animals had yet been relocated to the new barn. David had arranged for Rachael's mamm to bring her special wedding dress when they returned for the family meal that was planned since last week. Only her mamm was privy to David's plans for the romantic secret wedding in the barn.

As the morning waned, Rachael and her family prepared the buggies to drive her entire family over to the Todd's home. This was to be the very first gathering of the two families since their engagement announcement. Rachael was feeling a bit weary from waking so early, but was far too happy to succumb to sleepiness. As the buggies approached the Todd's farm, the Todd family was already outdoors, setting the long table for supper. Rachael and her mamm went towards the house to help Mrs. Todd and Gloria with the meal, and the men and boys toured the farm, and played ball. Just as Rachael thought it was time to summon everyone back to the outdoor table, her mamm took her aside, and presented her with the dress,

"Mamm! Why did you bring this? David and I have not set a date yet! Did you bring it to show Mrs. Todd?"

"No, dear daughter. Today is the day you must wear the gown. It is your wedding day," she cried, and Rachael stood aghast at the surprising news,

"How did you know? Did David plan this whole thing?" she exclaimed.

"Yes, of course he did. What else would you expect from him? He loves you more than words can describe, as I'm certain you know! Hurry on up, and put that dress on," she ordered,

"no more time to stand about with your mouth open." And mother and daughter laughed as they dressed Rachael for one of the most important days of her life.

Dusk had fallen, and the men had been busy hanging lanterns all around the barn area. The barn itself was lit with only candlelight and the flower garlands. It was a picture of pure beauty, yet simple as can be. Rachael's daed escorted her towards the barn. Once inside, she marveled at how ethereal it all appeared, and then she looked at David who stood proudly ready to make her his wife. The preacher performed the ceremony, and they all headed towards the long and fully laden table under the lanterns and stars. Everyone took their seats, and a hush fell upon the table as David remained standing,

"Today has been the happiest day of my life. Rachael cared for me like an angel, and now we are married! But before we sit down to this delicious looking meal, I have something very important to announce, both to our family members, and to my dear wife."

Rachael came to stand beside him, for this was something she and David had already privately discussed, but she had not known that tonight was the night to announce his big project. Her heart was overflowing with pride and love for the man that she nearly lost to a tragic accident. Gott had spared him, and allowed them this special life. She was extremely excited to start this chapter of their lives together, especially since David was ready to announce their plans,

"Today, family, and Pastor Robert, we stand together in joy instead of sadness. It is important to note that Rachael was almost made a widow before she even had the chance to be a married woman. Too many women in our community have lost husbands to early deaths or tragic accidents. Rachael and I are beginning a charity that will serve the women that have suffered such a devastating loss. We will be living in town near Pastor Robert, and we shall be coordinating our efforts with neighboring communities, including our Englischer neighbors. The services we will provide will be open to any who are in need whether Amish or not. It is our way of thanking Gott for his blessings, and allowing us this very special day!"

There was clapping and cheering from around the table, as Pastor Robert recited the grace. It was certainly a night no one would ever forget, and it was the beginning of the beautiful promise that David had made to his beloved Rachael so long ago in the meadow.

AMISH SWEETHEARTS

ERICA FANNING

Isaac Yoder couldn't remember a time in his life when he felt so alive. It wasn't his first Sunday night out with the other Amish teenagers. In fact, he was coming up on his 18th birthday, but this night was different. There was singing and Bible reading, as well as fellowship with the young women to find a potential mate, but this time was different. His best friend since 3rd grade, Miriam Hershberger, was there for the first time. She had just turned 16. He had liked some of the other young women well enough, but when Isaac saw Miriam that night, with the twilight coming in through the church windows and the candlelight dancing off of her loose golden locks that never really stayed in her head covering, he suddenly had different feelings for her. He might have imagined it, but he was sure she had looked his way a few times that night, and it was more than just a friendly look.

His friend Joshua noticed it too. "Look at Miriam over there. She looks beautiful." He had leaned closer so that no one else could overhear. Isaac nodded. "I know how much you like her." Isaac scoffed lightly. Joshua slapped him hard enough on the back to take his breath away. "Go talk to her!"

Joshua Hostetler was Isaac's best guy friend. Isaac, Miriam, and Joshua were nearly inseparable. Even though Miriam was two years younger, she always presented herself as the oldest of the three. Even in schoolwork, Miriam could have been two grades ahead, but her father wouldn't allow it.

Miriam's father, Jacob Hershberger, was absolutely opposed to Isaac courting Miriam. Had Isaac asked yet? No, but the men in the fields talked. Many times Isaac was sure they thought he couldn't hear them, but he heard every word: Jacob desired for his eldest daughter to marry none other than Isaac's friend, Joshua. Her father was insistent that he knew what was best for his daughter. Jacob only allowed Miriam to come to the Sunday singing because she had incessantly begged him to let her be a part of the youth group since her two best friends had both been there for two years. Rumor was that Joshua had already started dating Miriam, but when Isaac asked him about it, he denied it. Tonight was proving that more than any words.

The Amish (who call themselves Plain) have what they call *Rumspringa,* or more literally, "running around." It's a time for youths ages 16-22 to find a suitable spouse. There is a common misconception that it is also a time for Plain youths to experiment with the English (non-Plain) world. Though they have the option to do so, *Rumspringa* is more for finding a spouse than for experimenting with the world. However, Isaac had been entertaining the idea of leaving the Plain community to join the Army. The only people who knew of this were Miriam and Joshua. There was something about being in the Army that really intrigued Isaac. He had seen soldiers come through their community on tourist trips and had asked them what it was like. Many of them had been overseas and seen things Isaac only dreamed of: new worlds, new cultures, and new people. The only thing really keeping Isaac in the comfort of his community was the potential to date and marry Miriam.

"I think I'm going to ask Miriam if I can take her home," he finally said to Joshua.

Joshua chuckled, "If you hadn't said that, I would've done it."

Isaac smiled wryly. Ever since they were young, Isaac and Joshua were always in competition; to many it was even a surprise that they were such good friends. Isaac believed it was because of Miriam they were such good friends. She had broken up more than one fight and was always keeping the peace between the three of them.

"This is one thing I won't let you win."

"What? Why not?" Joshua looked affronted. "We can't even have a little friendly competition for a girl? And especially for a girl we've both liked since we were 8?"

Isaac shook his head. "Nope. I thought we had discussed this. I'm the best option for Miriam."

"Oh really? Well Mr. Hershberger doesn't seem to think so. You and I both know the rumors are for Miriam and me. I'll make a deal with you; if Miriam accepts your offer, then you can have her." Isaac shot him a skeptical look.

"That's really nice of you... but why would she say no?"

"Well, my friend, you may not realize this, but Miriam likes me better." Isaac rolled his eyes.

"Why does the world always revolve around you and your stories of a love triangle?"

Joshua held up his hands. "Hey, it's what sells these days. And I would know, since I work at a bookstore in town. But don't worry, I'll let you try to win her hand. But you and I both know, it's her father's heart you'll really have to win. So good luck." Joshua slapped him on the back again before rising from his seat. "I'm going to ask Rachel Swartz if I can take her home." He winked as he walked away. Isaac watched him leave. Rachel Swartz's father was just like Miriam's: very stubborn and wanting one person only for his daughter. In this case, that person happened to be Isaac Yoder. It occurred to Isaac in that moment that Joshua may have been trying to make him jealous, but you can't make someone jealous that doesn't even have feelings for a certain person.

Isaac sighed as he built up the courage to stand up and walk over to where Miriam was sitting. As he moved toward her, the girls around her steadily grew quieter and began speaking in more hushed tones. "Miriam," he half-squeaked as she turned to look at him. He cleared his throat before finishing his request, "May I take you home tonight?" There was suddenly a flurry of giggles from the group sitting around her.

"I'd love that," she replied sweetly. He offered his hand to help her up and began leading her toward his buggy. He had recently purchased the buggy from Rachel Swartz's father. Although "purchased" would be the wrong word, since Caleb Swartz gave it to Isaac as a sign of good faith that he would "make the right choice" in his future wife.

Isaac pushed all of that out of his mind as he helped his best friend into the carriage. He ran around the other side and got in and off they went toward Miriam's home.

About halfway there, Miriam finally spoke. "You can't take me home."

This caught Isaac off-guard for two reasons: one, she had been completely quiet until that point and it had startled him; and two, it didn't make sense.

"Why not?"

"Because," she barely whispered above the clopping of hooves, "my father will be angry with me if I bring anyone other than Joshua Hostetler home."

Neither of them spoke for a few minutes, but Isaac led the buggy toward their favorite secret spot. This spot was known only by Isaac, Miriam, and Joshua. The three of them had found multiple places to hide away from the adults over the years. This particular place was right on the edge of the community, very close to a busy road, but far enough away that it wasn't so distracting in the quiet moments. This spot was Isaac's favorite hiding spot. It was in that spot that he had tutored Miriam in her arithmetic and helped her learn how to read. It was where they had read countless Nancy Drew books in secret, and also where they would get together to talk about their fears of the future and their hopes for each other. Before life got to be about who to marry and where to work, this was where they felt the most at home. Isaac felt it was the best place to go since it had such a deep meaning for them.

As they approached the spot, he had to get out of the buggy and lead the horse to a tree where he could tie the beast up safely. Isaac picked a tree that was far enough away from the road that passersby wouldn't see the buggy and accidentally think something had happened. They were hidden quite a ways into the wood for that.

Isaac helped Miriam out of the carriage and led her through the wooded area to the clearing. It had been awhile since Isaac had been here—almost a year at least—but everything was just as he remembered it: a small circular clearing, not more than 10 feet around with three small logs around the edges of the clearing and a flat-top rock to make the fourth sitting spot. There was an evergreen tree on the north side of the clearing, and that was where they had hidden many of the "forbidden" Nancy Drew books in wooden boxes Isaac and Joshua had made in their free time at home. The entry point was on the south side, and there was a small piece of cloth with Miriam's initials on it. Isaac was never really sure why she had done that, and she had never explained herself... and that was just another reason why he loved her; she did things without anyone's approval.

The sun was almost completely gone, but the Sunday night gathering would last for some time before anybody's parents would start to get suspicious about where Isaac and Miriam were. "Remember the last time we were here together?" Miriam asked. Isaac smiled, recalling that day as if it had just happened yesterday.

"We all showed up here at the same time. You had had a rough day at school and Joshua and I just needed a break from working. We thought we could get away and just play some cards, but then you showed up." He looked into her eyes. "It was in that moment that I realized I wanted to marry you someday."

Miriam furrowed her brow as she said, "That was the day? I was a mess; I was crying like a baby—"

"No, you were wailing like an old widow." They laughed at the thought. Miriam sat down on a log.

"Yeah I was." She chuckled, but to Isaac it sounded like the birds were waking up in the morning. She began speaking again, but he could only focus on her features. Her beautiful golden hair was now freely flowing, as she had taken her head covering off after declaring that they couldn't go to her house. What she said was only mildly important to how she carried herself and how mesmerizing she was. Her green eyes fit well into her oval-shaped face. Her petite nose reminded Isaac of one of the glass baby dolls that his mother had on display at home. When she smiled, all he saw was perfectly white teeth behind full pink lips.

"Did you ever realize how beautiful you are?" He didn't even stop to think that she might have still been in the middle of a story.

"What?" She seemed a little surprised at the sudden outburst from her friend.

"You're beautiful," he declared.

She looked at him awkwardly then said, "I thought this was the time when we were supposed to talk all night long. We are basically dating, right?"

"We are talking. You're telling me stories, and I'm telling you how beautiful you are."

She scoffed. "The whole situation sounds a little one-sided to me."

Isaac shrugged. "Well, it worked. You're not telling me stories anymore."

Miriam gasped in feigned offense. "Oh, I see how it is. You don't even want to listen to how Mr. Troyer came into the shop and flirted with me? It's really quite entertaining." Isaac laughed with her. This was going to be a great night.

"Go ahead and start your story again. I'll be good and listen this time, I promise."

That night was the springboard for a whole slew of secret adventures together. Isaac and Miriam grew closer together in ways they didn't know was possible. Isaac felt like he was on the highest mountain and nothing could touch him. For the next three weeks, they would meet in their secret spot late in the evenings and talk into the middle of the night.

One night in particular, the conversation led to the future.

"Hey Isaac," Miriam started. "What do you think about the future?" She looked at him. "Do you think we end up together?" He thought long and hard and then chose his words carefully.

"I don't know what the future holds for us," he spoke slowly. "But I do know one thing." Isaac looked deep into her eyes. "I don't want to live my life without you." There was a long moment of silence as they looked into each other's eyes. Finally Miriam broke the silence again.

"Do you want to go into the Army?" Isaac looked away. The answer was, he really wasn't sure. And he told her as much.

"Those Nancy Drew books made me want to explore the world outside, and the soldiers that came through here recently made me just want to travel. So, I'm not sure if I would just travel or join the Army."

"Well," Miriam began. "You know how our Lord feels about war."

"Does He really feel that way though?" He looked up at her again. The moon was very bright that night and it made Miriam look almost angelic. He continued with his thought despite the minor distraction. "There's war and fighting all throughout the Bible. Even Jesus Himself said He came to bring a sword, and to bring families against each other."

"Do you really only want to fight because you think it's OK? Is that how you're justifying all this in your mind? Any time you take a life, that's blood on your hands that you'll have to answer for."

"Yeah, but Miriam, it's not just about the killing. It's about saving the lives of those that can't fight for themselves. Aren't you always going on about how you want to do what's right and bring justice to people's situations?"

Miriam was incredulous at this point. "Of course, but not by getting myself involved in some war and killing people. I want to help people *here,* in my community. I want to tutor young children... like you and Joshua helped tutor me." Her face softened as she leaned toward him, her voice almost a whisper. "Isn't that enough?"

Miriam was so close, Isaac would've agreed with anything she said at that point. He could feel her breath on his face, smell her sweet, natural scent. "Yeah," he breathed out, before leaning in to close the distance between his lips and hers. As soon as their lips touched, something like a fire shot through Isaac's body and he instantly wanted more. Every nerve in his system and every hair on his body seemed to be standing at attention, but in the next second, he was left breathless and confused. Miriam had pulled away.

"No," she stated firmly. "I can't." She stood to leave.

"Wait, Miriam." Isaac stood to follow her. "Don't leave. I'm sorry." He wasn't sure why he was apologizing, since he didn't really start the whole ordeal.

Miriam kept walking toward Isaac's waiting horse and buggy. "I need to leave. Please take me home."

"Wait, Miriam," he said again, more firmly this time as he reached out to grab her. She spun around, and what Isaac saw stopped him. She was crying.

"Please just take me home. I can't be with you. I can't keep playing this game of pretending to be into someone but really loving someone else."

Isaac released her arm. "Who else are you interested in?"

"It's not who I'm interested in, it's who my father *wants* me to be interested in. I can't keep pretending anymore." She looked into his eyes, and he had this sinking feeling that this might possibly be the last time he would get to talk to her for a long time. "Isaac, I love you, but if you want to date me, you *have* to get permission from my father." She turned around to continue walking toward the buggy.

"OK," he said finally. They had reached the buggy by then. "Give me a week." He reached out his hand to help her up, but she ignored it.

"Fine," she stated flatly. "Now take me home."

Three days later, he was met by his younger sister on his way out to the secret place to surprise Miriam.

"Where are you going, big brother?" Rebekah asked.

"Out," he answered curtly.

"To see Miriam?" That stopped Isaac in his tracks. He spun around.

"How did you know about that?" He asked defensively. Rebekah was 14, but sometimes Isaac swore she was his second mother. Sometimes she even caught onto things faster. This was one of those times. "You can't tell Mom and Dad about this."

"Why shouldn't I?"

"Because," he responded quickly. "If you do, they'll tell Miriam's parents and then I won't be allowed to see her anymore." Rebekah rolled her eyes.

"It's not me you have to worry about. It's all your little friends out in the fields. Everyone knows you and her have been leaving the singings together every Sunday night. Besides, it's not like his forbidding you to see her has actually stopped you. So where do you go?" She almost became a detective in that moment, and Isaac thought for sure she would pull the answer out of his eyes. As if to make sure, he looked away.

"It wouldn't be a secret place if I told you," he stated. He looked at his little sister, and in that moment, he was proud of the woman she was growing up to be. Whoever the man was that would have the honor of marrying her would be the luckiest man on the planet.

"Please, don't tell Mom and Dad. I'll tell them when the time is right."

"And when is that gonna be?" She crossed her arms as if she'd just made the best argument all day. *Wow, she is sharp,* he thought.

"Soon, I promise. I have to talk to her parents first."

"Well you better do it fast or else one of the guys in the field might let it slip. Mr. Hershberger is said to be making his rounds any day now to check on his affairs. I just worry about you, Isaac. That's all." She uncrossed her arms as her face softened. "Please don't do anything you'll regret."

Isaac smiled at her. "I promise, little sister. Thank you." He gave her a hug before heading out the door. Tonight was the night, he had decided. He would ask Miriam for forgiveness for the other night. Then he would ask if they could, in fact, go steady. Not only that, he was going to talk to Mr. Hershberger if she said yes. He felt as if he couldn't get his horse to go fast enough toward the secret spot. Sometimes the old beast had a mind of his own. As soon as he was within a shorter walking distance, he got out of the buggy and began coaxing the horse through the grass into the woods before tying it hurriedly on a tree and rushing to their spot. He had a few preparations he wanted to make before she arrived, since they had agreed on meeting at sundown after Miriam put her younger siblings to bed. He had his grandmother's wedding ring on a chain around his neck that his mother had given him on the night he turned 16.

"When you find the one you want to marry, give this to her as a token of your love," Isaac's mother had said. "Explain to her what this symbolizes, and above all, don't let her go."

These thoughts were running through his head as he walked quickly toward the clearing. As he got closer however, he heard voices. Two of them to be exact: one male, and one female. His heart started racing. Who else could know about this place? Of all the years he and his friends had been coming, not one other living human being had ever been here. He decided to hide behind one of the bushes just outside of the clearing, as he couldn't see into it because of the way he and his friends had designed it over the years. He listened intently, hoping he'd be able to recognize a voice.

His heart felt as if it dropped into his stomach and he felt all color drain from his face. He recognized both voices, and they were none other than his best friends', Miriam's and Joshua's. And they sounded happy. In a panic, Isaac forgot about stealth and all of the things he had been planning for that night as he rushed out from behind his hiding place and burst into the clearing, startling his friends.

"Isaac!" Miriam exclaimed, jumping up from her seat. "I didn't expect you tonight!"

"Didn't expect me?" He suddenly couldn't think clearly. All of the words and thoughts in his head were suddenly very jumbled. *What was going on here?* He wondered. If this is what jealousy felt like, he suddenly understood why Joseph's 10 brothers threw him into an empty cistern in the book of Genesis. "How could you not expect me? We've been meeting here almost every night for the past three weeks! I told you I had something special I wanted to tell you, and you *promised* that you would be here, alone!" Isaac's voice had reached a pitch he didn't even know existed, not to mention the volume it had gone up to. He ran his hands through his hair as he began pacing around the small clearing. He tried to get his heart rate and voice back down to a level that wouldn't arouse suspicion from anyone close by. Joshua, who had been struck mute until then, finally stood up.

"Look, we didn't mean anything by it. We were just hanging out. You can still have your time—"

"How long has this been going on?" Isaac addressed Miriam, interrupting and ignoring Joshua. His voice had now become almost calm. "Is this because of what happened the other night?"

"What?" She asked. Her eyes widened, suddenly remembering. "Oh... no!"

Joshua sighed, exasperated. "Isaac," he began. "I've tried to tell you from the start. It's about getting to know her *father.* He's the one whose heart you really have to win. He doesn't want some guy he barely knows to marry his daughter."

"Some guy he barely knows?" Isaac practically roared, forgetting all pretenses of trying to keep quiet. "I grew up with her, the same as you! We've been over to her house multiple times and had the *same* conversations with him."

Miriam attempted to be the peacemaker. "Guys, please—"

"Oh, have we now?" Joshua shouted at Isaac. "So you know what Miriam is struggling with right now? That she's still in shock from your kiss the other night? The one that *you* initiated? You know that her mother is sick and she simply can't bank on someone whose heart is set on 'traveling the world' to help take care of her. How could you be so selfish?"

Those last words struck Isaac to the heart. He looked at Miriam pleading, hoping that Joshua was wrong and that all of this was just a bad dream. Had she really been putting on a pretense all for him? "Miriam? Is what he's saying true?"

Miriam stuttered but seemed to be without many words. She looked scared, but she finally nodded.

"Well Army-man," Joshua said smugly as he folded his arms. "Looks like you didn't know her as well as you thought. Maybe you should just forget this ever happened and run on home to your little fantasy land." Just then, there was the sound of men rushing in their direction. *So much for not drawing attention,* Isaac thought, mentally kicking himself for letting his emotions get so out of control. He turned to Miriam.

"Come with me."

For the third time that night, Miriam stuttered.

"Miriam, I love you. I don't know if I could go on living without you. You mean more to me than the whole world, and there's nothing I wouldn't do for you." He moved toward her, but Joshua got between them.

"Stay away from her," he warned, his eyes bright with jealousy and hurt. The voices were getting closer.

Finally Miriam spoke a clear thought. "At one point in time, I may have loved you, but I don't know if I can love a man that can't even stand up and fight for what he thinks is right... unless it's at the end of a gun."

So this whole ordeal wasn't even about the kiss. It was about Isaac's obsession with war. Most people would've taken this as a cue to change, but Isaac took it differently.

"I'll come back for you." He looked into Miriam's eyes one more time. Those beautiful green eyes. "Then you'll know that I really do love you." She furrowed her brow in confusion.

"What? Where are you going?"

"Yeah," Joshua added, also confused. "Where *are* you going?"

The voices were almost upon them now. In a flash, he took off his grandmother's wedding ring. The thought passed through Isaac's mind that the night wasn't meant to go like this. But it was too late for that. "This is a promise, that I love you and I will come back for you. Give me three years."

"The last time you promised a certain amount of time to her, you did *nothing* to deliver on that promise," Joshua reminded him with a hint of vitriol in his voice.

"We'll see," Isaac said with what he hoped was an air of mystery in his voice. Really he was just scared of the choice he was about to make.

At that moment, the first man in the search party came through the clearing. Isaac took off running deep into the woods and farther away from everything he held dear. He thought he heard someone running after him, but Isaac was the fastest man in the community, even Joshua wouldn't be able to catch him.

For the first time in his life, he felt like he was making simultaneously the best and worst decision of his life.

And it was already killing him.

"Sgt. Yoder!"

For the first time in his life, Isaac was less than excited to have those two words in the same sentence.

"Yes sir!" He addressed his commanding officer with as much respect as he could muster. Staff Sgt. Queener was his least favorite person as of late. Ever since they had gotten into a firefight with the Islamists in Iraq a few weeks prior to returning, he would find everything wrong with anything Isaac did. Queener blamed Isaac for the fact that they had gotten into the fight in the first place, and although Isaac didn't claim Queener was wrong, he also wasn't about to take responsibility.

It was our last sweep of the town, Isaac had written down in the report. War wouldn't have been so bad if there wasn't so much red tape afterward. *We were on our way back to base when a little girl came running up to me. About 10 of us were on foot to make sure if there were any civilians, we wouldn't scare them with our big vehicles. The little girl couldn't have been more than 5 or 6, and she began speaking Farsi much faster than I could translate. I asked her to slow down, but asking her seemed to have the opposite effect. At this point, the convoy had stopped, and Cpl. Lanning had begun trying to coax me that we needed to get moving. As long as the convoy was stuck, we were practically sitting ducks.*

No sooner had he said that then shots rang out from the nearest building and instantly the little girl who had just been standing in front of me suddenly had a chest full of bullets.

At this point, Isaac had had the hardest time finishing the debrief. He couldn't understand how anyone could allow someone to die like that and continue to live a normal life. One of the psychiatrists he had talked to after coming back had said Isaac would have to find a new normal, but Isaac didn't even know what normal was since he'd left his Plain ways behind to join the Army. He did know that he was responsible for that little girl's death... as well as the death of his best friend.

Instantly a firefight broke out in that little town, but all I could do was take cover. I was the group translator, so my number one priority was to stay alive at all costs. However, I also happened to be a sharp-shooter because of my upbringing, so I managed to take a few terrorists out without anyone realizing who or what hit them.

Taking the lives of those men was nothing compared to the loss of that little girl, or my best friend, Cpl. Lanning. It wasn't until the smoke had cleared that we realized we had lost him within the first few seconds of the fight. One of those first shots had been toward him, and it was a direct hit.

Lanning's life and that little girl's were what got him, not any of the terrorists' or anyone else that might have died as a result of Isaac's actions. He still had nightmares about that day. He ran through scenarios every second of the day in the back of his mind. He remembered seeing how scared the little girl was and desperately trying to decypher what she was saying. He remembered hearing the rushed tone in his best friend's voice and—after thinking about it every night for the past month—he realized he even remembered Cpl. Lanning's last words before getting shot in the throat.

"Come on man, don't do something you'll regret."

It wouldn't have been so chilling if it wasn't so close to the last thing he had heard his sister Rebekah say to him almost 3 years ago.

"I said, did you hear me, Sergeant!?"

Queener's voice snapped him back to the present.

"Yes, sir!"

"This is a disgrace! How could you just put in a request like this? You're one of my best men!"

Maybe Isaac would've listened if he hadn't already had this conversation with himself in his head. Every decision he'd made in the past two and a half years, he'd made after deciding if hearing Staff Sgt. Queener's voice was worth it.

In this case, it was because the request that Queener was so upset about was a request to leave the Army. He needed a signature and recommendation from his commanding officer before he could get out. His time wasn't up, but it had been almost three years, and he had promised Miriam Hershberger three years. He wasn't about to renege on his promise, even if he wasn't even sure she had really waited for him.

In the middle of Queener's rant, he finally said, "I have to go see about a girl, sir."

That stopped Queener in his tracks. "Oh," he said stupidly, after a few moments. "Well, why didn't you say that to begin with?"

The next few weeks of paperwork went by at a turtle's pace, but finally Isaac was out and on his way back. He hadn't looked back at his Amish life in three years, except to think about Miriam everyday.

What would it look like now that he had had a taste of freedom and the English life? Would anybody recognize him? Would anybody care? Would Miriam care? Did she keep his grandmother's ring? What about Joshua? Did he tell everyone what Isaac had done, or did he just take Miriam for his own? He suddenly had an insatiable ache to see his friends and to give them the biggest hug ever and just weep on their shoulders.

"I should've stayed to fight," he had told his first and only friend in the Army, Cpl. Lanning. "I loved her, but I didn't know how to fight."

Lanning had leaned back to look at the ceiling before stating simply, "I don't know, the whole system sounds fishy to me. You were either going to win her or not, and if she didn't really love you, then what was the point of even 'giving it a try?' I don't know about you, but I think you leaving was the best decision you could make. Don't feel sorry for the fact that you may have just won her heart by becoming the most unreachable man she's ever known."

Isaac wasn't really sure where Lanning had gotten all of his wisdom from; Isaac had asked him one time what he thought about God and the Bible, but Lanning had just laughed at him.

"That stuff is for little kids and the weak at heart! You're better than that, Yoder."

Despite what Lanning said, Isaac held true to his faith. It was the only thing that got him out of bed in the mornings... especially after coming back from war without Lanning. He tried to push that out of his mind as he was getting closer to his hometown. Like a wave, he felt all of the shame and regret from three years ago wash over him. Coupled with the recent loss of the little girl and Lanning, the pain was almost unbearable.

He didn't know why, but he decided to stop at the secret spot, maybe to get the last look at his childhood memories. No matter how today turned out, Isaac decided, he was leaving at sundown, with or without Miriam. Not surprisingly, the clearing was empty. It was the middle of the workday, so Isaac was pretty sure it would've been void of life.

Walking into town was going to be the hardest part, Isaac had decided. Because he left, and without saying goodbye to anyone but Miriam and Joshua, he was sure a lot of people would be upset about him leaving. There weren't a lot of people at the shops because they were all in the fields or in the nearest English town working. Out of habit and homesickness, Isaac went to his parents' shop. Before his eyes had even adjusted to the dimness of the store, he was tackled by the biggest hug he had ever received.

"OH, Isaac!" It was Rebekah. Instantly, Isaac returned the hug and they just held each other and wept. Finally Isaac broke the hug.

"Where's Mom and Dad?" He asked. Rebekah looked down and began crying again.

"They're gone, Isaac." She looked back up at him. "The pain of you leaving was too much to bear. Mom passed away within a month, and Dad just passed last week.

That wave of shame and guilt suddenly felt like a tsunami of emotions. He needed to sit down. Rebekah must have noticed the color drain from his face, because she quickly pulled him to the nearest chair and began fanning him.

"I'm sorry, Isaac," she finally whispered. "I tried to find out where you were to tell you, but you made yourself almost impossible to find."

"No," Isaac finally forced out. "I'm sorry... for leaving you alone like this." He looked up at her quickly. An idea was forming in his head. "Come with me."

Rebekah was shocked. "What? Come with you? You're not coming back?"

Isaac shook his head. "I came back to get Miriam, no matter what it takes."

Rebekah looked away as her face flushed.

"What?" Isaac prodded. "Tell me."

"Well," Rebekah seemed to struggle with the right words. "She's supposed to get married tomorrow... to Joshua Hostetler."

All feelings of guilt suddenly left as adrenaline kicked in. He stood up quickly. "Little sister, I need your help."

Rebekah looked unsure, but nodded. "Okay," she said. "I'll go with you too."

Isaac was actually taken back by that. "Really?"

"Yeah, it's not like any of the available guys are all that interesting here anyway. What else is there? This shop?" She laughed sadly. Isaac moved over to her.

"Hey," he cooed as he enveloped her in his arms again. "It's alright. If you don't want to leave, I understand."

"It's not that I don't want to leave," she admitted. "It's that I don't want to forget about my parents."

Isaac pulled Rebekah back and looked into her face. "Hey. As long as we're alive, our parents will never be forgotten. We keep their memories alive by the way we live."

"But would our parents want us to just leave our community like this?"

"The better question would be, do our parents want us to be miserable in this community?"

Rebekah seemed to realize that Isaac had a point. Their parents had always been huge proponents of their children doing whatever they wanted, as long as they were happy and followed the Lord.

"Following the Lord is a lot easier out there than it is in here," Isaac added almost as an afterthought.

Rebekah furrowed her brow in suspicion. "Okay, Mr. Mind-reader. I don't need another Mother in my life."

They laughed. Isaac didn't realize how much Rebekah's laugh really did calm his nerves.

"Okay," he said, more seriously. "We need a plan to get to Miriam."

"I have an idea, but it requires a lot from you."

Nothing could be worse than the rest of my life without Miriam in it, Isaac thought as Rebekah began laying out her plan.

It was finally here. The moment Miriam had been raised and trained for all her life. Her parents were so excited, but she couldn't help feeling just a little empty. It must have shown in her face because her mother brought it up.

"Honey, what's wrong?" Ruth asked. "Today should be the happiest day of your life, but you look like your favorite doll just got stolen."

"Mama, it's just not the same without Isaac here. He was one of my best friends too, and it's hard knowing that he can't be here to see this."

"I know, honey," her mother said sympathetically. "But it might just be better this way. You know Daddy never liked Isaac much anyway."

Miriam sighed heavily. That didn't make it any better, but she had to give credit to Ruth for trying. She wasn't supposed to get married until later that evening, because there were a lot of preparations going into this day. She wouldn't even be in her dress until midday, when they would start preparing her makeup and hair for the ceremony later on.

"You look beautiful," a familiar voice said. Miriam spun around to see who it was, half hoping it was Isaac Yoder, since she had just dreamed last night that he had rode into town on a horse and swept her away from this whole world. It was her father, Jacob, and he looked the proudest she had ever seen him. She smiled wide.

"Thank you, Daddy," she curtsied playfully as he moved into the room to give her a hug.

"I'm so proud of you, Miriam Joy," his voice sounded husky, like he was holding back tears. "So proud."

She pulled back a little bit to look into his face. It occurred to her that this was the beginning of a new era for her father, since she was the first of five girls that would be getting married over the course of the next ten years.

"I'm just glad Mama gets to be here to see this," Miriam said thankfully.

"Mmm," was all Jacob could force out, as tears were now flowing freely. He kissed his eldest daughter on the head and left the room. Miriam wasn't sure how she would feel if Isaac did show up today, but after seeing her father cry, she didn't know if she'd be able to bring herself to leave him like Isaac seemed to do with so much ease three years ago. He had made it look so easy, but she could hardly bear the thought of leaving her family alone for one minute.

Or so she hoped.

That hope is what Isaac and Rebekah were doing their best to play on. Rebekah hadn't become extremely close to Miriam over the past few years, but she knew enough to know that Miriam would most likely leave with Isaac if he showed up and asked her to. True to Lanning's prediction, Miriam had grown more fond of Isaac... even to the point of intentionally waiting exactly three years to get married.

Isaac saw it as a test of his love; would he be willing to potentially ruin his best friends' wedding if it meant winning the love of his life? Without a thought, Isaac knew the answer was yes. He had made too many mistakes in his life to let this one try to rule him.

Rebekah told Isaac that Miriam would be going to the flower shop alone right before heading back to her house to get dressed for the wedding. That would be the best time to talk to her.

True to predictions, Miriam walked into the flower shop alone. Isaac made no time at all in getting there. He was destined to do this long before the wedding.

"Miriam Hershberger," he declared before his eyes had adjusted from the sun outside to the darker interior. By the time they had, he realized he was standing face to face with none other than Miriam.

In another lifetime, he might have taken a step back and apologized for standing so close to her. This was not another lifetime. For the first time in three years, Isaac smelled that sweetness emanating off of her. She had pulled herself so close to him just like that night in the secret spot, but this time Isaac made the move. He pulled her in tight and kissed her fully on the lips. It was like fire and ice, burning and refreshing all at the same time.

It was just like Miriam's dream! Not only had Isaac returned, but he was there to take her away. This kiss confirmed it. She pulled herself as close as she could to him, determined to never let him go. Finally, he pulled himself away, drinking in every detail of her with his eyes.

"Come away with me."

"What about Joshua? And my father?"

Isaac was undaunted. "What about them? Are you living your life for them... or for yourself?" His voice was barely a whisper, but to Miriam it seemed as if he was shouting. He was shouting, *I love you! I desire you! Come away with me! Never look back!*

"Do you know what day it is?" Miriam asked him. He smiled.

"May 28th. Three years to the day that I told you I would be back. You waited for me."

"I knew you would come." She pulled the ring off from around her neck. "This is for you; it's a symbol of my undying love and devotion to you. I don't know why I ever treated you the way I did, Isaac. I—"

He put his finger on her lips. "Whatever happened in the past is in the past. Now is the only moment worth living for." He looked deep into her eyes. "Will you come with me right now?"

"Yes!" There wasn't a second thought in Miriam's mind. She didn't care what anyone thought or what would happen to her. She was in the arms of the man she had always truly loved.

Getting Miriam to leave without saying goodbye to anyone was the hardest thing to do, so Isaac compromised. They both went to see Joshua.

Joshua was at the church getting preparations ready. Normally he wouldn't be doing anything, but he wanted to surprise her. Then he turned around and saw what seemed like two ghosts coming down the aisle toward him. As soon as Joshua saw them coming, he knew that his life with Miriam was over. He had finally been bested by his best friend, Isaac Yoder. They not only looked happy, but also like they were about to leave.

"You're leaving with my girl?" Joshua said with a twinge of hurt in his voice.

"Come with us, Joshua," Miriam pleaded. Joshua only shook his head.

"A love triangle might sell in the world of books, but it doesn't work in real life." Joshua put his hand out toward Isaac. Isaac took it. "You bested me, old friend. Now don't mess it up."

Isaac smiled. He could tell by the way Joshua responded that even he saw this coming. "Thank you, old friend. I do wish you would come with us, but you're right about the whole love triangle. Besides, I think Rachel Swartz still likes you." Isaac winked. Joshua only smiled.

"Get out of here before I change my mind. Besides, you can't just take the whole community with you. There would be no one to make awesome tourist attractions to intrigue soldiers coming back from war."

Isaac had to laugh at Joshua's attempt to be funny. He was taking this better than Isaac expected, and that was all that really mattered in that moment.

"Goodbye, Joshua Hostetler."

"Goodbye, Isaac Yoder. Don't get too crazy out there. Goodbye, Miriam. I hope your life is all of the happiness you're wishing for and more. You deserve it."

Miriam smiled. "Thank you so much." She went to hug Joshua, but he pulled away.

"Don't make this any harder than it already is," he warned. Now Isaac could see that he really was hurt. It broke his heart that it had to end like this, but he was glad that Miriam would be with him.

"I'll write to you from time to time," Isaac said. "The Hardy Brothers need some new adventures anyway."

They shared a moment of camaraderie before Isaac and Miriam turned and walked out of the church and into their new lives.

They met Rebekah at the secret place. "I talked to your dad," she addressed Miriam. "He cried. He wanted me to give you this. I guess he always knew this was coming." She pulled out a small book: her grandmother's diary. She had never been allowed to open it, but she had been told stories from it.

"I guess he was going to give it to you at the wedding, but since he'll never see you again..." Rebekah trailed off.

There were a few moments of no talking before Isaac finally said, "Let's go. It's time to start our new life together."

He smiled as he put his arms around his sister and his lifelong love. As bittersweet as the parting was, it was the best decision he had ever made. In that moment, there was nowhere else he'd rather be than in the arms of the woman he loved.